The Wondrous Library

Her heart picked up the pace of its beating as Gran observed the treasure trove of antique artifacts the shelves held. Books filled with anything other than someone's personal diary or journals were expensive things, and rare outside the homes of a few rich nobles. Gran had once taught in a university that felt blessed to own seven. There had to be at least sixty tomes here; and all of them once the property of Istipol. They must be priceless!

But money was not Gran's purpose here. It had never been a priority to her, and she wouldn't begin worrying about it now. She had come here looking for some knowledge of the symbol on the medallion, driven by some idea she had yet to fully form in her mind. Why did she believe that the library would be of use? It was at least a century out of date. Something had brought her here. There was something here that she was meant to find, or to do. Perhaps something she was supposed to read. She hoped so. Reading had always been a pleasure of Gran's and something she had not been able to really indulge since she left the university.

Not sure where to begin, she walked to the left wall and reached for the first book on the end. A faint crackle of energy and a light shock came from the touch.

"Ach!" she screeched, far more offended than hurt. "So I am to be killed with lightning? I was brought here just to die, like as not," she grumbled, looking at the floor to see if she had passed across any carpet on the floor, but seeing nothing there but pure white sandstone. Thinking that perhaps it was now safe, Gran reached for the same book once more, and was again rewarded with a minor zap of pain.

Growling, Gran stepped back from the shelf and thumped the book once with the base of her walking staff. The wood trembled from the coursing electricity that passed into it. Surprised and not a little frightened at the power, Gran dropped her staff and stepped back further, wringing her hands to ease the tingling.

"I understand you now," she grumbled, looking around the room for some hidden guardian. "I'm not supposed to touch that book."

No one replied, so Gran tried the next book in line and was shocked again. She moved up a shelf and then down one, receiving a shock each time. Moving down to the far end of the original shelf, she again felt the bite of a spark.

Throwing her head back, Gran shrieked her frustration and moved to the bookcase on the back wall. She hesitated before touching a book there. Would she receive the same type of shock, or possibly even a worse one? Perhaps here she would be burned by a ball of fire. Was she missing something? Had she forgotten something important?

BlackWyrm Books by Trevis Powell

Albrim's Curse
The first book in the Were-War series

All young Albrim wanted to be was a master bowman like his father. Then a savage attack on his home cost him his family, his arm, and his humanity – all at once! Crippled and contaminated by the Curse, his beloved Gran leaves him in the care of Mute, a giant warrior dedicated to protect-ing humanity from the depre-dations of the Quarg. Albrim does what he can to assist his master and redeem himself. But can a werewolf ever really recapture his humanity?
[Epic Werewolf Fantasy, ages 14+]

To learn more about upcoming novels, visit us online at www.blackwyrm.com

Gran's Secret

by Trevis Powell

A BlackWyrm Book
Louisville, Kentucky

A BlackWyrm Book
BlackWyrm Publishing
10307 Chimney Ridge Ct, Louisville, KY 40299

Printed in the United States of America.

ISBN: 978-0-9820067-9-5
LCCN: 2009912802
Cover by Jeff Easley
Edited by Andrea Howe, Blue Falcon Editing

First Edition (as "No Hero"): September 2006
Second edition: March 2010

To Sandy;
my one and only

Prologue

The victory howl of the Were was suddenly answered by a chorus of dozens more from the forest, which was in turn followed by the sounds of war horns and distant shouts. Quarg war horns. Dozens of Quarg war horns.

The shouts and war cries of hundreds grew deafening as the humanoids descended upon the highway with their wolf allies. The Were's surprise lasted only a moment and then he moved into action, crossing the carriage and looking down for the person he had come to kill, then growling his pleasure at the sight of the old woman attempting to escape on that side. Gran was moving as swiftly as she was able, but the seconds bought by Conn's death had allowed her only a few steps towards safety; a safety that no longer existed with the coming of the Quargs.

Chapter One

The little old woman plied the broom across the rough boards that made up the porch of the Bucket of Ale with a vengeance normally reserved for young boys doing a poor job at weeding her cabbages. Muttering under her breath, she occasionally repeated her mantra of 'Like as not' as she made every effort to drive the straws of the broom through the new wood. Whatever was upsetting her was not readily apparent, but the locals were avoiding her anyway.

She was dressed like most of her neighbors in clothing of un-dyed homespun cloth worn in layers and footwear made by wrapping a long strip of leather around the foot and tying it off with leather strings. Old she was and old she looked; her hair gray without even a hint of another color and her face was deeply wrinkled. Her back was slightly bowed but her step still contained a spring and the life behind the faded blue eyes still blazed like a beacon. Her neighbors considered her peculiar and said many things about her behind her back; not the least of which was that she was 'healthier than she ought to be.'

Springtime was well along and Gran's thoughts were never far from her grandson. It was nearly a year now since the attacks by the wolves and she worried for Albrim every day. Sending him away had been necessary, she knew that, but she missed him terribly. If that big brute that lived in the forest harmed him even one bit more than was necessary, Gran would see to it that he regretted it.

"Give him the back of my hand or the flat of a scrub brush I will, like as not," she told herself in smug satisfaction. Gran looked out for her own as best she could and everyone she knew was her own in one way or another.

Life in Cobble was not the same, nor could it ever be for Gran and the other survivors. When Lord Ferule had moved them here it had been a time of excitement and adventure for most of the settlers. Before coming to Cobble most of them had been nothing but peasants or serfs, but here they were given a small plot of land that was their own, providing they lived on it for ten years and labored in the Lord's own fields. It wasn't a great deal of land but enough for a hovel and a good-sized garden. More than any of them had ever owned before.

It had seemed like a wonderful dream to most of the peasants and even some of the freemen such as her son Borel. He had brought his family here to better their lives and now Borel was dead at the hands of a Were and his unholy pack of giant wolves. Her grandson was dead as well for all her neighbors knew and Gran was all alone.

So many changes had come to the little village. More settlers had arrived, just as Lord Ferule had promised, and the empty or damaged homes had been quickly rebuilt and occupied. On the north edge of town the foundation had been laid for a stone barracks where a company of Lord Ferule's horsemen would soon form a permanent garrison and a watchtower had already been constructed. Gran had ordered the village's alarm bell moved up there but already the members of the local militia were forgetting to man it, most days. The improvements were too little and too late to Gran's way of thinking.

No sign had been seen of wolves in the area since the day the Were was killed. Some might say that was a good sign, but not Gran. Wolves were natural creatures and should be seen occasionally. The lack of the bigger wolves and Weres was a good thing, neither were natives and had no business in Aldragal, but no wolves at all meant that someone was keeping them away. Someone or something that had influence over the beasts.

"There's another one out there, like as not," Gran told herself. She agreed with herself as well, acknowledging the brilliance of the observation.

Finally recognizing that further sweeping was of little use Gran went back inside the tavern to oversee the preparation of the evening meal. By a twist of fate, the owner of the Bucket of Ale and his entire family had perished in the Were attack despite their business being the only place where anyone had survived. Lord Ferule had taken ownership, as was his right as the land owner, and sent word that Gran should take over the business in his name. Whispers were that Lord Ferule didn't want the family-less Gran to return to his home estate; he'd had enough of her as a younger man when Gran had cared for him. Either way Gran was glad of the opportunity; it both gave her something to do and kept her in a position to keep up with the news.

Consequently Gran's assumption as proprietor saw the sale of ale in the tavern drop by more than half as the old woman wouldn't hesitate to throw out anyone she believed had drank too much or simply should be home in bed. Overall, however, the business was more profitable than ever as Gran's experience in the kitchens drew in customers from all of the nearby villages and she wasn't above bullying travelers that might have tried to travel a few more miles before dark into spending the night. Lord Ferule accepted his profits and otherwise stayed away, knowing a good thing when he saw it. Some said it was out of fear of Gran.

With the death of Yogarn a few weeks past, his weak heart finally gave out, Fat Happ was permanently assigned to the position of Village Reeve and Gran was now a member of his council. Many considered Gran the only member of the council, but this was not true. In reality there were others appointed to the post and even Gran recognized that they were integral parts of the council and gave them and Happ every opportunity to agree with her before she did as she pleased. No one could complain about the results; the village had never ran more smoothly. The first winter after the Were attack had been difficult. Many crops had rotted in the fields without enough workers to harvest but the dramatic drop in mouths that needed to be fed offset this somewhat, and the strict rationing program designed by Gran had seen to it that all had enough.

Her switch held ready, Gran watched as two of her helpers prepared the night's meal of roasted mutton and boiled beets, the second being the last of the previous year's crop. Small and shriveled, they weren't much to look at as far as beets went but Gran would see to it that they tasted good. Once they were properly boiled soft she intended to deep-fry them in bacon grease. It was a trick, she called it a recipe, that had fooled many young boys into eating their beets.

The back door slammed open, allowing entrance to a small blond boy of five. He ran once around the big preparation table before honing in on Gran and rushing to her side.

"Gran, there's a stranger in town!" he said excitedly. It was his task, given to him by Gran herself, to report all such amazing occurrences directly to her.

"There's a good lad, Tobe. Where did you see this stranger?" she asked, digging into the pocket of her apron for a suitable sweet for the boy.

The boy was bouncing in his excitement. "He's at the smithy. I guess he don't know old Yogarn died."

"Like as not, Tobe, now off with you," Gran said, offering the treat. Tobe grabbed it and was gone out the door in a flash.

"Law, Gran, but that boy doesn't walk anywhere," laughed Mily.

"He's a good boy," stated Gran, discarding her apron as she left the kitchen.

Gran picked up her walking stick and hobbled down the steps of the porch to the cobblestones of the square. One of her first acts as an advisor to the Reeve was to bully poor Happ into replacing the cobblestones stained by the blood spilled here around the tavern. It was easy to see which ones were new but the survivors of the attack didn't need that reminder; Gran certainly did not.

Her son had died in this very tavern and her grandson had lost an arm to the same Were that had killed Borel. Now Albrim suffered from the Were Curse and was safe nowhere. Nor was anyone safe from him.

Gran hurried as much as she cared to. At her age she felt that even those who didn't know she was coming should have the patience to wait for her arrival. Strangers were still a rare occurrence even after a winter spent bringing in new settlers and men-at-arms. Both of those had come from the same estates that the first settlers of Cobble had originally hailed from so in truth they hadn't been strangers at all, merely old acquaintances and even blood relations for some. Whenever a true stranger wandered through Gran took care to meet them, to see who it was and what business brought them so far off the main roads. She was expecting trouble to arrive eventually, and today might just be early enough.

The quiet smithy quickly came into view despite Gran's less than robust gait. Cobble remained a small town after all. A bay horse stood waiting patiently before the building, seeming to favor one hoof slightly even while standing still. The animal was shaggy and unkempt, still carrying its winter coat despite the lateness of the season. To Gran, this was a sure indication that the traveler had come from the far north or across the mountains where snow still held.

Above the building a faint line of smoke was beginning to rise into the air. Someone had started a fire in the smithy. A faint rattle of metal on metal came to Gran's old ears; someone was looking through Yogarn's tools.

She stalked up to the smithy as if the building belonged to her. In truth it did in her mind, as did everything in her town. A fire had indeed been built in the forge and there was the stranger sorting through the tools of Yogarn's trade.

"There will no thieving around here, stranger," Gran stated loudly, ensuring that anyone in the nearby homes would hear her, just in case there was trouble and she needed help. Not that Gran would ever admit that there was any trouble she couldn't handle.

Slowly the stranger's head lifted, the wide brimmed hat had effectively blocked Gran's view of the stranger, as had the ankle length black cloak and expensive looking black leather boots. But now the face was visible and Gran found herself gazing upon the most capable looking woman she had seen since the last time she saw her own reflection.

The stranger was wide of face and broad of shoulders with cheekbones that stood out prominently and a chin that extended to a sharp point. To call her ugly would have been too harsh but she was decidedly plain. Her hair was almost yellow, the color of a golden squash, Gran decided. It was the eyes of the stranger that caught her attention first. They were so blue as to almost hurt to look upon them and proved instantly that the stranger was not from Aldrigal; nor anywhere else this side of the mountains. Gran knew immediately that this woman was dangerous. Now she had to decide exactly to whom she was dangerous.

"I'm no thief," the woman growled, her hand reaching for a dagger hanging prominently on a belt. The move was casual, meant simply to show that she was capable of defending herself and not actually a threat; what did she have to fear from a frail little woman like Gran?

Gran met her gaze square on. "I didn't say you were a thief, I just said we don't allow it," she snorted, not intimidated in the least to all appearances.

The stranger stared hard for second before releasing her grip on the dagger. "Like I said, old woman, I'm no thief. My horse needs a shoe and the smith doesn't seem to have been here for a while, so I was going to tend to it myself."

Gran nodded her acceptance. "Fair enough. It is true we've been without a blacksmith for a while now. He died only a few weeks ago, but he hadn't turned his hand to a bit of work since last fall."

Stoking the fire the woman pretended to be only half listening, but Gran knew differently. The position of her shoulders, the set of her chin; she was very much interested in what was being said.

"Some type of fever?" the stranger asked.

"No, bad heart," Gran said, sitting on one of the chairs that once were filled by the various town loafers when Yogarn still lived. No one had bothered to drag them in out of the weather.

"Oh," the woman said, trying to disguise her disappointment. Gran let the silence drag on for some time until finally the stranger felt the need to break it.

"Heard tell of some bad times up this way," she said, still stoking the fire.

Gran wouldn't give in that easily. "Yes, the cabbages didn't do well and the wheat was blighted from too much rain last summer. The Harvest was shorthanded too, made for a hard winter."

The stranger looked up from the forge she was tending. "Are you daft, old woman? I meant the troubles you had with the Cursed!"

Pretending to be surprised Gran answered, "Oh! Those troubles. Yes we did. Powerful bad troubles. Lost a son and a grandson to the wolves. Terrible thing for a woman of my tender years to have to deal with."

"Tender years? You're an ancient crone that would make the world a better place with your death. You're just in the way of someone younger," the stranger said dismissively.

Gran was shocked. It had been some time since anyone had talked to her like that. Since the death of her last husband at least.

"Better old and gray with the wisdom that brings than young and stupid with all its ignorance," she said, not exactly calling the stranger stupid but implying it with every word. She saw the stranger's face redden slightly but the woman failed to take the bait. Gran could see the woman's temper, however, and it was not far from the surface. Gran wasn't sure why she was baiting the woman, but there was information here that she wanted, if not needed.

"More than wolves, old woman. You were attacked by one of the Cursed. A Were."

"So we were and many died, as I said. Why do you care?"

The stranger moved about her task, again feigning indifference.

"I intend to be in this area for some time. If there are Weres around, then I should know about it, so I can prepare to defend myself."

Gran laughed, choosing that moment to leave. She knew that she wouldn't get far.

"What of the Weres?" demanded the woman.

Pausing Gran looked back. "There was one and I killed it. That was nearly a year ago now and no more have come around since."

The stranger held silent for a moment, obviously disbelieving the older woman's claim. An old woman such as this crone killing a Were? Highly unlikely without magic and this feeble hag didn't look like a sorceress. Finally she asked, "What of those bitten by the Were?"

"There were none who survived. I burned and buried them all."

Eyes narrowing slightly, the woman turned away from Gran and back to the forge, adding more wood to the now blazing flames.

Gran left the smithy moving even slower than normal. Her mind was spinning furiously, replaying each word spoken by the stranger and every small movement of her body. She was a suspicious sort, Gran knew. The woman was here for a specific reason and wouldn't be deterred by a lie no matter how convincingly told. This stranger was here looking for those Cursed in the attack last spring and had somehow determined that one with the Curse had survived. Regardless of her source of information, she wouldn't be easily dissuaded from whatever her task was.

This was the trouble that Gran had expected.

Chapter Two

The tavern was virtually silent now having just begun that period of time between the last of the customers staggering home and the first rats making tentative forays out for food. Sounds there were; the popping of the building settling on its foundation; the gentle rumble of a kettle left too close to the fire, the ragged snores of the woman passed out beside the fireplace, the soft footsteps of the proprietor as she shuffled around in her woolen slippers checking windows and doors to be certain of their security, but none were intrusive or broke the quiet contemplation such a late hour demanded.

As a tavern it was small; with only three rooms; a common room and a kitchen with a storage room off it on the ground floor and a loft above whose bare plank floor was covered in straw-filled mattresses for the comfort of the occasional guests. There were no stairs, only a ladder and no chamber pots were provided so the back door was usually left open when there were guests to access the well-maintained path to the distant outhouse. No one was availing themselves of the loft on this night so the old lady in her gray shawl and simple, worn ankle-length dress wasn't concerned about being overheard.

Gran enjoyed the tavern when no one else was there. She loved the smoothness of the floors and even the odors, not all pleasant, that had become a part of the place. The fading scent of the mutton roasted earlier, a hint of herbs, the smell of ale from a leaky barrel in the storage room, the faint aroma of unwashed people that had embedded itself into the very furniture. This was her home now, and to all those who knew her she seemed content to live out what little remained of her life here.

Running a tavern had never been something Gran would have strived for. She'd always been content raising her children and grandchildren by maintaining a good sized garden and earning a coin now and again by nursing her neighbors through diseases, births, and injuries. But to her surprise she found it enjoyable and there were tasks enough to pass the time of day; plus she was at the best location to be among the first to hear all the gossip a small village such as Cobble could generate.

Vert sat at the table and cried from a combination of grief and fear. Though a young man he was a veteran of a battle with a Were backed by giant wolves and had unflinchingly faced both to defend his neighbors without regard to his own life. Tonight he had faced something that had clearly been more than he could handle.

Gran looked over the young man, her heart softer to his plight than he would have believed. She'd been the midwife that birthed him, as she had for so many others in the village, and she loved him as her own. His hair was light and his face splotchy, he'd never be considered truly handsome, but he was a steady lad and useful. Gran already knew that he could keep his mouth shut. She searched her heart for the right words; the best way to help the lad get past his fright and to somehow ease his conscience as well. None of this had been his idea and she'd had to bully him into doing it but it had been necessary. Through all her many years of life Gran knew the best way to handle such situations; her wisdom was locally legendary, and she knew precisely how to sooth the young man.

"Shut up, boy, or I'll switch you!" Gran stated, bolting the back door of the Bucket of Ale. "It's done now and you survived. You're out of danger completely, like as not."

He tried to stifle his tears but they refused to stop flowing. They were tears of relief to his mind, justified by the horror he had just experienced.

"Gran, it was just awful. That was a devil-woman, I tell you!"

"Now you hush, Vert, like I told you to. You did what you had to do, and no more! She's gone and you're shut of her."

"But Gran you don't know what it was like," he sniffed, drinking long from the mug of cider Gran placed before him. His hands were still shaking.

"Never mind the whimpering," Gran scolded. Vert had charged a Were armed only with a pointed stick and now he was scared of a woman. If she had Vert's size, strength, and youth, Gran wouldn't be scared of anything. Well, she admitted to herself, she wasn't scared of too awfully much as it was. "Tell me what she had to say!"

Vert's crying eased, but occasional sobs would still shake him as he replied. He, and everyone else in the village, viewed Gran as their adopted grandmother. "Well I did like you said, Gran, I kept buying her drinks all evening until she finally started to act friendly."

Gran sniffed. "I know that, fool; I was the one bringing her the drinks! It was me that slipped the four-leaf into them too!" Four-leaf was a local herb known to increase the potency of alcohol. Adding a few dregs to a mug of ale would give it twice the inebriation power. Gran had added a lot more than that.

"I wasn't drinking anything but cider, and she still almost out-drank me!"

"I know that too, boy. You're soft." Gran had been bringing his cider watered down just to be sure. The last ones were nearly all water. "But knowing that you're weak will keep you away from strong drink, which will make you a better man. Now tell me what you learned."

Vert rubbed his face, gathering his thoughts. He knew that Gran had been close by all evening so it was unlikely that the old woman hadn't heard everything. Still, he had lived his whole life obeying the old woman and didn't even consider refusing.

"At first she was mean, saying terrible things about me and Cobble and how much she detested us all. She said that I smelled bad but what can I do about that? If I don't tan hides I don't eat! Not with father and mother dead from the wolves."

"I know what you do for a living, Vert. It's an honest profession and nothing can be done about the smells. Now tell me what the woman said."

"Well, she started out really mean, just like I said, but after a few hours she started to become... interested... in me. It was awful, Gran!"

"Keep talking," Gran said, pulling a switch from somewhere and laying it on the table. Not close enough to be threatening but clearly visible to the man.

Vert sobered some at the sight of the switch. "After another hour or so she turned all maudlin and started talking about how much she hates Weres and how they killed her whole family and now she spends her life hunting them down and killing them."

He took another long pull on the cider. "That's why she's here, she heard about the Were attack last year and came to see if any were still around. She's convinced that the one you and Sir Garen killed wasn't alone or maybe before it died it had bit someone and given them the Curse."

Suddenly the tears flowed again; stronger than before. "Gran, did we do the right thing with Albrim? Did we do the right thing?"

Gran brought the switch down across Vert's hand in a stinging strike. "Of course we did! He died and we burned his body. What else could we do?" she said, rolling her eyes meaningfully around the room. Despite her precautions Gran knew that she could never forget that Cobble was a small town and people were easily overheard. Once a secret was out, it was out forever and would soon spread from mouth to mouth and village to village across the kingdom. It was her grandson that had been bitten by the Were the year before and Gran had seen to it that the boy would have a chance, a small one admittedly, to have some sort of life beyond being hunted as a killer. Gran, with the help of Vert and a woodsman named Tomo, had taken steps to make everyone believe that Albrim had died. In reality the boy had been taken to receive help; to perhaps even overcome the Curse that now tainted his blood.

"Yeah," Vert said, taking the old woman's hints before nervously changing back to the original subject. "By the end of the night, she wanted to sit in my lap, Gran. I wanted to say no because she's bigger than me but was afraid she might pull a knife!"

"She didn't, Vert. I saw to that. She'll sleep the night through right there on the floor. We could put her hand into the fire and she still wouldn't wake up until morning! Now stop worrying about her and tell me everything that she said."

"She might be faking!"

"I kicked her more than once, hard," Gran groused. "If she's faking I'm a mule."

Vert's imagination was swept up in a vision of the wrinkled old crone's features slowly dissolving into those of a mule, and decided that at least in temperament there would be little change. A mule would have fewer wrinkles.

Snapping back to himself, Vert replied, "Well she's talked to everyone in town and is convinced that there is another Were somewhere out in the forest. She doesn't suspect anyone from here has the Curse or else we would have had some mysterious deaths or at the least be missing some sheep."

"Well thank the Fates for that much, anyway." Gran said thoughtfully, pouring herself a mug of the fermented cider. She didn't water hers down; she had kept her mind clear all evening, just in case, but could afford a little treat now with the stranger, whose name was Jarma, unconscious, and therefore temporarily harmless in the next room.

Setting the mug on the table, Gran sat across from Vert and waited for him to continue. He did so, repeating every word the stranger had spoken throughout the evening to the best of his memory.

"She says that she's going south to search tomorrow, and then she's going over to Spicer to scout around. I think that was a lie. She was trying not to say it but I got the impression that she's awfully interested in Hemlet. I think that she's really going there, thinking that any Weres in the area might want to move into a deserted village. She supposed it might be a good place for a Were to hide out for a while, since no locals will go there any more after all the deaths."

Gran cackled. "Good for her. Let her go up there and root around. She'll find nothing but some burned shacks and a squad of Lord Ferule's horsemen!"

Vert was surprised. "I didn't know Lord Ferule had a garrison in Hemlet."

"He doesn't have one, not exactly. They're part of the garrison from Spicer, but one squad stays in Hemlet for a week at a time. They sweep the area for wolves just in case a second Were thinks of the same idea as your lady friend."

Vert looked insulted. "She's not my lady friend! I wouldn't have even talked to her if you hadn't made me."

Gran smiled smugly. "So you say, but everyone in the village saw you buying her drinks tonight and then her perched on your knee later. It'll get around, young Vert and they'll be trying to marry you two off, like as not."

Vert turned green now. "Gran, I been sparking Jelli Noggil for six months. If this gets back to her she'll drop me sure!"

Still cackling, Gran slid her switch back into her apron pocket. "I know who you been sparking, Vert, don't you think that I don't. I'll take care of Jelli for you. She's a bright girl and I'll make sure she knows you were working for me."

"Thanks Gran, that's a relief."

"Of course she'll still make you pay for it, like as not."

Vert smiled weakly, hoping that Gran was teasing him but pretty sure that she was not. You could never be sure with Gran.

Gran sent the young man home and saw to the barring of the door behind him. With all the torches out and both of the ancient oil lamps trimmed, Gran settled down by the fire with her mug of cider and, with her feet propped on the stranger's head, contemplating everything she and Vert had learned about the woman.

All in all, Gran decided that the stranger remained dangerous on many levels but for now she was content to leave the woman to her own devices. Temporarily, at any rate. However, the woman remained a distinct danger to Albrim and not just in finding him and killing him herself. While possible, it was highly unlikely, considering where Albrim was and who was watching over him. More likely to happen was the woman picking up some news or information concerning another Were that Gran herself suspected still remained at large. If the woman did discover the second Were, even if she managed to kill it herself, the news would spread quickly and swarms of adventurers and Were killers would rush to the area and then Albrim would be in danger. One Were had brought a lot of attention to Cobble and a second would bring far, far more.

Gran sipped her cider and considered drawing herself something stronger. She was quite prepared to do whatever she had to do to protect her grandson but didn't like her choices. For now she was content to do nothing, but if the stranger became too suspicious, asked the wrong questions of the right people, or searched the wrong area, Gran knew what she would have to do.

Chapter Three

Children followed the workmen around everyday, playing games nearby as the well was dug and on hand to inquire about each and every aspect of the job; sometimes asking the same question again and again. Each of the workmen were family men and took the youngsters in stride, utilizing them on occasion to bring them a drink of water or perform some other minor task to help the children feel important. Fat Happ, the Reeve of the village, came by periodically to check on the well-diggers progress. Despite being treated to a new jump-roping song created by the children just to make fun of him, Happ only laughed along with them and allowed the children to remain. So long as the children remained to watch the men dig they wouldn't be getting into trouble somewhere else.

Gran was in a foul mood and that sort of news passed through the village more quickly than a brushfire fled through dry brambles before a stiff wind. Unsure of the cause of her ire the people took normal precautions and simply avoided the old woman; keeping inside with their doors closed when possible. Some of Cobble's more notoriously lazy citizens decided that this would be a great day to go hunting, just in case Gran's anger was aimed at, or could be diverted to, themselves. Only the men digging the well and the children playing nearby were outside and Gran seemed to have no interest in any of them.

"Like as not we'll all die of thirst this winter," Gran grouched as she stalked the village streets like a hunting cat, disdaining the well-diggers efforts and completely ignoring that fact that it was she who had 'witched' the location for the new well.

Gran gave Yogarn's empty smithy a good glare as she passed. Word was that a Journeyman from Spicer had just been elevated to Master status and would be sent to Cobble to take over the business after his upcoming marriage. In the meantime the broken hoes and were piling up and endangering Gran's cabbages. This angered Gran as well but had nothing to do with her present foul mood; that was attributed to nothing but waiting.

She missed her grandson terribly. Albrim had been a special young man and Gran had had high hopes for him; still had for that matter, though her ambitions for him had been altered completely.

Naturally Albrim would never have children; Gran well knew that those with the Curse were sterile. Another brood of youngsters carrying her blood had been a pleasure she had anticipated; now she would have to find another option for that. Following in his father's footsteps as a bowyer had been Albrim's dream, and Gran had supported that as a good bowyer could provide himself a comfortable living, but with the Curse in his veins and only one arm he would have to find another way to earn his keep.

His life had been altered so much that even surviving was not assured; there were many who would kill him for his Were blood alone, and Gran couldn't even blame anyone who did. Weres were, most often, mindless killers that murdered indiscriminately. Little better than the animals they resembled, a Were rarely developed any sort of control over their passions. Most often this was because they failed to live long after revealing themselves, although some who did survive just didn't care about controlling themselves and fully embraced their animalistic sides.

Waiting was worse than anything. Gran had seen to Albrim's needs; he was safe, would be fed, and his problems with the Curse would be dealt with in time. However Gran was not privy to any updates on her grandson's situation, at least not any she could count on. Every month or so Tomo checked the hollow tree as she had instructed and only once since sending Albrim away had Gran received any word about him. Even then a crude drawing of a man-like wolf chained to a rock was certainly of no comfort.

And even if she were not waiting for news of Albrim then Gran was still waiting; that woman Jarma was around someplace, sticking her big nose where it didn't belong. It was only a matter of time before she began asking the right questions of the right people despite the layer of subterfuge Gran kept laying down. Mostly she just spread rumors and told lies but she could foresee a time in the future when she might have to be more direct in her actions. Gran didn't want to go that way but she knew that she might not have a choice if she wanted to protect her grandson.

Walking around the blackened square that had once been her son Borel's workshop, Gran crossed the one-plank bridge that spanned the ditch and inspected her personal garden. It was much larger than last year's had been. Lord Ferule paid for laborers to handle the work as all the produce would be used to supply his tavern but it was Gran who owned the little plot of land. She studied the arrow-straight lines of tiny green plants just beginning to show as she considered her options.

Jarma, the stranger, had made no secret about her purpose here. She had tried to be subtle but Gran knew that she was looking for any signs of a Were. Did she suspect that Albrim survived the battle after being bitten? Perhaps; Gran wasn't sure despite all her work. Even if Jarma did not but believed someone else in the area had survived with the Curse or that there was a chance another Were might come here like the first it was bad news for Albrim. Time was the only cure for Jarma's curiosity; if enough passed by with no credible rumors or sightings of Weres in the area the woman would eventually have to leave.

Gran knew that Jarma was reporting to someone as well. The stranger's written reports had 'fallen' into Gran's hands and even though the actual information in the missives was well disguised Gran knew what Jarma had discovered; so far not much of anything, but the woman still hung about the Cobble area looking for more and that was what was really bothering Gran.

Moving around her son's house Gran made sure that anyone watching her saw her inspecting the roof for leaks. She made a slow circle around the dwelling until she was out of sight of most of the village before she turned and darted into the copse of woods. Moving as quickly has her bent back would allow, Gran walked until the green spring brush hid her from all view and then sat upon a tall stump, her feigned bad temper melting away although her worries remained to plague her.

It was one of her favorite spots. Sitting on this stump had once been a pleasure to be looked forward too as she had utilized this very spot to tutor a younger Albrim in his letters on nice days. The trees were tall and grown thickly together overhead, leaving the ground in perpetual shade. Brush, taking advantage of Albrim and Borel's absence, had grown up between the trees and the odor of honeysuckle was thick. Gran tolerated the brush because now she valued secrecy more than a pleasant view or unhindered breeze when she came here.

"Gran?" came a soft call. Not much more than a whisper it still carried far enough and was pitched high enough for the old woman to hear.

"Come on in, Tomo, we're alone," she answered, not whispering but not speaking loudly either.

With a whisper of branch on leather the woodsman slid through the brush to join Gran, dropping to a squat near her stump. His boots were stained with new blood; he'd obviously butchered something recently, and he smelled like it too. A pair of flies began to circle him immediately.

"You stink like Happ's outhouse, Tomo. Don't you ever bathe?" she grouched, making a show of pinching her nose shut. Tomo only grinned.

"I butchered a deer, Gran, about two hours ago. It's great to be out here in the wild instead of on the Lord's estates," Tomo proclaimed, dropping a hide-wrapped parcel at Gran's feet. "I brought you a cut."

Tomo, like most everyone else in Cobble and the surrounding villages, had been born on the estates of Lord Ferule and hunting on his lands was forbidden unless you were a huntsman for the nobleman. Not that many of the peasants, Tomo included, had let a little thing like poaching stop them from feeding their families. In all fairness Lord Ferule had usually turned a blind eye to such lawlessness when crops were lean and winters long, but occasional examples had been made of those who abused the privilege. Out here in the borderlands, however, the deer were free for the taking year-round and many were glad to take advantage of it. Not only could the meat feed a family for some time but the hides could be traded for other necessities.

Patting the fellow's cheek Gran thanked him for the venison. "It'll come in handy Tomo, thank you."

Smiling as if he were a child being praised Tomo felt his face blush. Gran had a certain way about her; he always felt like a child when around her.

"No problem Gran, just don't go sharing it; that's for you. Let them other people buy their venison from me."

Giving his face one last pat Gran nodded her agreement; unwilling to ruin Tomo's good mood by reminding him that she didn't have enough teeth to do the venison justice and there were those in the village who needed it far worse than she.

"Did you visit the stump?" she asked, not only to change the subject but also eager to hear from Albrim.

"Yes Gran, and all I found was this." Tomo said, drawing a folded sheet of brown paper from inside of his shirt.

Gran accepted it reverently, ignoring the sweat stains and body odor that the paper reeked of and gently unfolded it. The paper was of very poor quality and was already beginning to fall apart from the sweat and the moisture of the stump before that but Gran found what she needed; word of her grandson.

The paper was a wanted poster; like many she saw daily posted on the wall of the tavern. This one in particular, or some variant of it, had hung there for more than a decade and she easily recognized the face of the lonely woodsman she had sent Albrim to live with. As usual the face was poorly drawn and even as a caricature barely resembled the man but Gran knew him. There beside the drawing but much lower on the page was a second, this one more carefully sketched, of Albrim's face. To most people this would have meant little but Gran knew it to be a representation of where Albrim stood in relation to the ranger; the boy had grown over the winter! That meant he was healthy and was on his way to recovering from the Phobee. It also meant that he was learning to live with his Were Curse at least well enough that the woodsman hadn't been forced to kill the boy; at least not yet. Gran took what comfort she could from that.

"Well done, Tomo, well done," she whispered, tears filling her eyes as she gazed on Albrim's face. A drawing wasn't the same as seeing him, she couldn't hug a drawing, but it certainly beat not knowing.

The drawing had been made with a piece of rough charcoal but the artist had taken care to fill in as many details as the flimsy paper could hold. A few small dots showed that Albrim was beginning to come into a beard; not so surprising when you considered the Curse, and his eyes were drawn open and clear so Gran knew that he was past most of the pain. Turning the page over she found another sketch of Albrim, this one showing the boy from the waist up. His right hand had been replaced with some type of metal contraption that Gran didn't recognize but obviously the ranger had felt that it was important enough to let her know about it. Albrim's left hand was shown holding a sword; so she knew that the boy was being taught to defend himself.

Although she wished she knew more about the contraption on Albrim's missing arm Gran couldn't have expected any more information under the circumstances, so Gran cherished what she had.

"He's doing well then?" Tomo asked. He had seen the paper of course but had only guesses as to what the pictures meant.

"Alive and well, my only blood kin," she whispered, roughly knuckling the tears from her eyes as she stood. "Good work, check again in a month Tomo."

"I will Gran."

"Good, I may have something for you to take back with you, so check with me before you go."

"Yes Gran," the man said, rising to his feet ready to leave. He had most of a deer carcass cached in the fork of a tree and wanted to get it home before a forest cat found it.

"Wait a moment, Tomo, I need something else from you as well."

Warily the woodsman squatted back down; the tone in Gran's voice had him more than a little nervous.

"You're good friends with that fellow that delivers the mail aren't you?" she asked without preamble.

"Yes, I know him well. We talk now again when he passes through."

"You mean you drink together. Say what you mean, Tomo, and stop dressing up your bad habits like I'm your wife."

"Sorry Gran. We meet at one tavern or another when we can."

"Would he do you a favor?"

"Uh, you mean like the 'favors' I do for you? Not likely, Gran, at least not where the mail is concerned. He's almighty diligent about his duties."

Gran sat back onto her stump and propped one elbow on a bony knee and a bonier fist beneath her chin. Tapping one finger thoughtfully against her pursed lips she thought long before speaking.

"Right," she said, taking Tomo's proffered arm to help her regain her feet. "That means we'll have to be a little smarter, like as not."

Tomo didn't like the sound of that.

Chapter Four

Warily the wolf slipped from the tangle of brush and sniffed delicately at the packed earth of the trail. It was a magnificent animal with dark furred tinged with red and a circle of white like a collar around its throat. Tall and powerful it would easily weigh as much or more than three normal wolves and was strong enough for a small human to ride it like a horse if anyone were brave enough to saddle it.

After a thorough inspection of the path the wolf lifted its nose to the air and sniffed the gentle breeze, then peered nearsightedly as it slowly spun in a circle; watching for any movement that might tell of approaching danger. It licked at its muzzle as it looked about; reveling in the taste of the blood that coated it from its most recent kill. Finally satisfied that it was alone and unwatched the wolf sat back on its haunches and began to tremble.

Flesh twitching, skin stretching, the wolf gave a soft moan of pain as the bones of its back and legs popped from their joints and began to lengthen. The process was not new to the wolf but it had never grown used to it either. Muscles bunched and clenched even as the fur withdrew or sprouted further depending on the part of the body it grew from, and after a few moments the figure of the wolf had been replaced by that of a hideous wolf-like man, who in turn faded away to be replaced by the form of a human.

Taking another wary look around the Were satisfied himself again that he was alone, and took a moment to collapse to the trail, gasping for breath after the rigors of the change.

As a human the Were was decidedly wolf-like with a thick covering of body hair and a long, straight nose. His hair was red, both the long, matted hair that hung past his shoulders and the thick beard that reached mid-chest, but there were strong similarities in color with that of the wolf he had been. Naked save for an amulet that hung on a chain about his neck, the man allowed his panting to ease along with the last vestiges of pain before he stood.

Smiling the man scrubbed a hand across his mouth, conscious of the blood that remained there after the kill. It had been a good hunt and he was pleased to have found game so quickly. While the animal had not provided much of a chase it had been a pleasant kill as it had kicked and snapped frantically at the end.

Lifting a pair of breeches from a nearby limb the Were slid them on as he replayed the chase in his mind. Mok's were not fast runners but their teeth were certainly sharp. A nice diversion from the pressures of his day.

Walking swiftly along the trail the Were soon encountered a sentry and soon three more. The men said nothing and only acknowledge his presence with a nod; too frightened to do any more; they knew what he was. Entering the camp soon after the Were marched immediately for the largest tent and was met by his aide before he came close.

"He's here," the young Quarg stated, his words garbled both by the difficulty of the language and the presence of the tusks that grew out from between his lips. His speech complete the aide sucked loudly to regain the spittle that invariably pooled in the corners of his mouth after speaking; an annoying habit that had seen him banished by his tribe.

"Good," the Were stated, moving around the aide and entering his tent. "I will see him once I have changed."

With a nod the Quarg darted away, his reluctance to speak was a benefit to the Were who despised unnecessary talking more and more the longer he lived with the Curse. Wolves were quite capable of communication but found very little reason to do so, and the Were sympathized with their reasoning.

Quickly the Were pulled on a tunic and his hated boots; he truly despised footwear of any kind, then plunged his head into the barrel of rainwater located by the front door of the tent before combing his hair and beard into some semblance of order with his fingers; the visitor was an important one. Satisfied with his ablutions he immediately left the tent and walked towards another well across the camp. Smaller but more ornate, with walls of silk beneath the canvas roof, this tent was only used when its present occupant made his infrequent 'inspections' of the camp. No one else wanted to use it because the silken sides let the night chill and dampness in too easily.

Pausing briefly the Were tugged the silken cord hanging by the door flaps and allowed the tinkle of the small brass bell to announce his presence before he pushed on in. The 'inspector' was technically his superior but the Were had no fear and only a minimum of respect for the man; there was another above him that gave the orders. If the Were meant to catch the other man by surprise he was disappointed.

Sparsely furnished the tent was almost empty; a camp cot, a small trunk made from cedar, a folding table and a stool made by a Quarg from fallen branches and the seat of a former stool represented all of the furniture and the new arrival had added little more. A leather pack atop the chest, a mud-spattered cloak was draped across it, and a thin leather satchel sat upon the table. Otherwise the tent contained only the man himself.

He stood in the center of the tent apparently working the kinks from his back after the long ride. Short, balding, and thin, he failed to cut much of a dashing figure despite his reputation. The man had been a successful assassin for more than a decade before accepting his present duties and the Were could respect that. Sniffing softly the Were searched the tent for any new scents and used his other senses to search for silver beyond the small pendant the assassin always wore. Satisfied that no threats were forthcoming the Were completed his entrance and held out one hand.

"Handrick," stated the new arrival, shaking the Were's hand with only a minimal display of emotion. Few would willingly touch a Were for fear of gaining the Curse. Even those who knew better remained reluctant but the assassin did not want give insult.

"Dirk," replied the Were, carefully grasping the smaller man's hand to avoid harming him. His strength compared to that of a normal human was difficult to judge and he wasn't used to holding back.

Without preamble the man called Dirk nodded, sat on the stool and began opening the clasps on the satchel. Handrick squatted easily across from him and waited patiently; neither were the kind to indulge in small talk.

With the buckles open Dirk pulled out a thick sheaf of parchments and efficiently separated them into several smaller stacks. The largest of these he returned to the satchel and then tossed it onto the cot before selecting a single sheet to read. Pursing his lips he looked up at Handrick before speaking.

"Report," he ordered.

Handrick gave a thin smile, invisible within his beard, and began. "Two more companies of mercenaries have arrived, bringing their numbers up to a thousand men. The Quargs are dragging their feet but I have two thousand of them on hand and more allegedly on the way," he smiled more broadly. "I will be forced to be more firm with them to obtain the warriors they have promised. The troops from Firth have been stripped of all insignia, just as the duke commanded, and appear as nothing more than better trained mercenaries, bringing my total command up to four thousand warriors, plus the wolves."

Dirk nodded and obediently wrote down the figures to report back to the duke.

"Fine, there are more Firth loyalists on the way and one other mercenary company I have hired. Also troops from Herth and Kelsten will be here after the harvest to augment your army."

"They're not an army yet."

"Perhaps not, but the duke is convinced that you can make them one."

Dirk shuffled his papers again and brought out one filled with neat columns of figures, bringing a silent groan to the Were's mind. Another discussion about supplies.

"Why do you serve the Duke of Firth?" he blurted, seeking to stave off the boring figures. "You don't have the features of a Firthian,"

Dirk paused, looked up once and smiled. "Neither do you, Handrick, yet you have served the duke longer than I. What are your motivations?"

Handrick shrugged. It was certainly no secret. "Weres have little opportunity at any sort of life. So as long as I serve the duke I can live a decent life; keep my Curse a secret from the population at large, and not have to live in a cave somewhere. He taught me how to control it, how to use it for my own advantage. Until something better comes along, I'm content to train his army."

"He 'taught' you by chaining you to a wall in his dungeon for several years."

"I don't begrudge him that; I might have preferred a better method but the truth is that chaining us down until we gain control of our changes remains the most effective way of dealing with Weres, short of killing us. I appreciate the effort."

Dirk smiled, carefully placing his figures upon the table. "My motivations are not even as pure as yours, my friend. I serve the duke for money; and protection. The more populated lands are no longer... inviting... for me."

Barking a laugh Handrick added, "You're wanted in the coastal nations so you had to flee to a backwater like Firth to avoid prosecution? I understand completely."

Not in the least offended Dirk joined in with the laughter. "That is it precisely. The duke recognized my skills and gave me duties far more challenging than slitting a throat or poisoning a goblet of wine; plus he did not order me put to death. I was glad to enter his service."

"Speaking of wine, you should join me in my tent later. I have some bottles that are slightly less than offensive. We could share a glass or two with my Lieutenants and discuss the coming war."

Dirk seemed surprised at the offer; an emotion he wasn't overly familiar, or comfortable, with experiencing. Still, there was no reason why he shouldn't or couldn't accept the man's offer; he had nothing to fear from the Weres so long as he served the Duke of Firth and he was nothing if not loyal. Besides; if Handrick decided to kill him or wanted to press him for information he had far more effective ways of doing so without resorting to getting him drunk.

"I accept your offer sir. Now we really should finish our discussion."

Thankfully the figures they spoke about were straight forward and took little discussion to complete. Caravans of grain and salted beef arrived monthly for the humans of the army and the Quargs and wolves provided their own sustenance, though they were forced to range further and further out from the western side of the mountains to do so. Blankets, clothing, and supplies to repair armor and weapons were already on site and enough of each arrived with each caravan to supply the new additions to the force. Everyone in the growing army was well fed; perhaps too well fed as Handrick had difficulty keeping all the men busy. Overfed wolves could be downright lazy but thankfully Handrick had firm control over the animals and they didn't really need to be trained. After all; they knew how to kill.

Mercenaries would only put up with so much training and fights between them and the regulars, and between them and the Quargs, and the Quargs and the regulars, were a growing concern. Handrick felt a certain amount of quarrelling was acceptable; even to be encouraged, but he didn't dare allow the fights to become deaths; he would need every man once they attacked. These details Handrick did not share with Dirk; they were his to deal with; the little assassin would not care to hear about it.

"That settles our business," Dirk finished, sanding the ink of his notes and then gathering his papers to put away. "I believe you mentioned something about a drink?"

Chapter Five

The western side of the Kenebruk Mountains looked no different than the eastern sides; thick with forest up to the tree line and forbidding snow-capped peaks atop tall slopes of blue above them. The Free Duchy of Firth had come into existence because of those mountains and the gold that washed down the River Firth found and harvested by the first duke. Small in size it had been historically rich in wealth, allowing it to avoid the grasp of larger, greedier neighbors. What they lacked in population they made up for with well-paid mercenaries and their people's hardy frontier zeal gave the Firthians a grit and determination the more 'civilized' nations lacked. Their freedom and independence had been bought and paid for with the blood of generations of Firthians and losing to an invasion never crossed the minds of the nation's leaders. Not until the gold from the river dried up.

It had been the father of the present duke who first ordered expeditions into the mountains. The Quargs and other humanoid tribes that lived there were fierce, and they were far from the deadliest denizens of the mountains, but Firth was desperate to find the source of their river's gold before larger nations discovered them destitute. Mines appeared all along the canyon of the River Firth but few produced more than a small flash of color and all were abandoned within a few years. Prospectors moved all the way into the mountains and discoveries were made; unfortunately for Lionel, the present Duke of Firth, nothing his people found had produced much coin for his treasury. He had gotten desperate. Desperate enough to risk an invasion.

Lionel took a long, deep breath of the cool breeze. This time of year most of Firth's weather came straight off the Kenebruks and today was no exception. The duke was thankful for the slight respite from the leaden heat of the day. His advisors, his legitimate advisors not those such as Dirk he kept in secret, were gathering to discuss Duchy business. He knew what they would report; coffers running low, income drying up, and would demands a halt to the capitol building projects he had initiated. They knew nothing of his overall plans and would not until the time was ripe. He simply couldn't trust them all and secrecy was paramount now.

But they were well-laid plans and the duke had absolute faith in their success. His father had been a master tactician and proved that fact against invasions by Carstoth, Bregantorn, and later an alliance of both. So thorough had been his father's victories that Lionel had not once needed to lead his own forces in defense of the Duchy but surely that peace could not last; it was only a matter of time before his more powerful neighbors discovered that Firth no longer had the money to raise an army of mercenaries. It had been his father who lay out the beginnings of the plans Lionel now intended to complete.

"Well, I may as well not delay," the duke announced. His manservant immediately stirred from his place in the shadows.

"My Lord?" the man asked, unsure whether he had been addressed.

Lionel smiled at the man's discomfort. A good servant; the man had no thought of concerns more pressing than the cleanliness of the duke's chamber pot.

"I go to meet with the council. Lay out my dinner attire and inform Her Grace that I may need to discuss a few points of law with her this evening."

The manservant smiled. They were back into his narrow view of the world. "Yes, My Lord," he intoned, scurrying off to heed his master's business. 'Discussing points of law' was a joke of the duke's; his reluctant wife should expect an amorous visitor this night. Little else did the duke require of her, or any of his late wives, beyond their dowries and the alliances their blood bought him.

It was a short walk to the council chamber but Lionel turned off one doorway short, choosing instead of a direct entry to enter the adjoining chamber first. It and the council chamber had been designed by his grandfather so that anything said in the main room would echo quite plainly into the smaller. Lionel was interested in what his advisors might have to say when he was out of the room.

"The mines at Dalwan are played out," came the voice of Baron Hagan, the only remaining noble with a working gold mine. "We've sunk several dry shafts; my engineers say the vein is finished."

"What of the shafts we've been sinking along the river? Some spots of color are still showing up; the deposits they are coming from must be there somewhere!" came the dry, nasally voice of Lord Kasten. A powerful man in his youth the dry little twig was now nothing but a hateful bundle of arthritic   spite.

"We've found nothing," boomed the deep voice of Adermon. The Chief Engineer for the duchy was obviously concerned; his father had served Lionel's father in the same capacity and was probably the most loyal member of the council. "I've sunk shafts up and down the riverbanks and found nothing."

"So the gold is gone? For good?" demanded the shrill voice of Lady Castanza. The mines in her lands had been the first to fail and the poverty her family was suffering was the worst among the major nobility of the nation.

"Gone? Not necessarily," replied Adermon. His family held a number of minor titles but nothing that matched with the other members of the council. "There is undoubtedly at least one major vein of ore left between here and the mountains; it's just finding it that remains difficult."

"And when it is found it will not be upon Castanza lands," came the whispered voice of Lord Kasten. It was unlikely that Lady Castanza heard it but the words were quite plain to the duke. Not for the first time he wondered if there were some magic involved in the construction of the rooms.

"How is our beloved ruler handling the loss of revenue?" questioned the husky voice of the Baroness Ezdrella. A formidable lady and, unless he produced an heir, Lionel's closest living relative. She would adore for him fail and if the nation went bankrupt she stood to gain the most. If Firth was invaded, she would be the most likely puppet ruler installed upon his death. Lionel had no trust to spare for his cousin.

"Very well," intoned General Nigel Intona, the nominal leader of Firth's military. A spit and polish warrior he kept his minimal forces in tight discipline but was practically useless as a tactician. If the need arose Lionel intended to perform those duties himself, unless Handrick was available and for the near future the Were-general would not be. "He has taken every precaution to keep our impoverished state from being known outside of Firth and has dipped heavily into his personal funds to maintain the core of the military and disbanded about half the troops. I have no idea how long he can afford to do it but I cannot complain to date."

"Not long," snorted Castanza. "He's raised the taxes but most can no longer pay even at the old levels. He'll be as destitute as the rest of us soon enough," she laughed, glad as always to share her misery.

Lionel smiled. The 'disbanded' units were those with the most loyal officers and he had dispatched them to the mountains. They were the core of his planned invasion. All the mercenaries there were hired using his personal funds as well, leaving him far worse financially than any of his advisors knew. As the council continued to speak the duke allowed his mind to wander; thinking of his careful planning and the forces he was building. If the Weres and Quargs continued to cooperate he almost had enough troops to accomplish the one thing that might save his nation if no new sources of income arrived. No one could be expecting so audacious a move as to have tiny Firth become the invaders for once.

Chapter Six

Tomo led the mule down the streets of Cobble, silently cursing the loud clops the animal's hooves made on the stones. Following along docilely behind the mule was a donkey, content as always to follow the larger beast. It was late and both moons had already set, leaving him to find his way through the town at times by feeling his way between the buildings. He wasn't concerned about becoming lost; so long as he was walking on cobblestones he knew he was in the town square, but stumbling about in the dark was no way to keep from being seen or heard. The few stars visible through the overcast sky helped him find the Bucket of Ale by default since the large building blocked many of them from view with its second floor.

Tomo knew for sure that he had found it when he tripped over the edge of the porch; no other building in town had anything like it. Skirting the edge, he led the animals down the alley to the rear of the building keeping a close eye on where the mule was stepping. Draping the lead animal's halter over a porch rail, he stepped to the back door and rapped quietly.

Before his fist finished its second soft knock the door was pulled open and Gran's silhouette was there, lit from behind by the banked kitchen fireplace. Scents of warm bread, cinnamon, and soap wafted out to envelope him in a mixture that pleased the nose and watered the eyes.

"I heard you already, you fool! Did you have to put cowbells on the donkey's hooves? You sounded like an army of Dwarven tinkers coming down the street."

"Sorry Gran, it was dark," was Tomo's whispered defense. He didn't bother to point out that Dwarven armies rarely were made up of tinkers, and that neither wore cowbells, at least he'd never heard.

"Help me up," Gran said, walking as softly as she was able to the side of the waiting donkey. Tomo wrapped his arms around her waist and easily lifted the old woman up to the saddle. She was light, but Tomo was surprised that she weighed as much as she did. Her pockets must be full.

Following her whispered instructions, Tomo handed Gran her walking staff and then retrieved a heavy pack wrapped in oilskin from inside a nearby barrel. It was bulky, unwieldy, and all he could do to muscle it onto the mule's back. Once in place, he had to tie it on to keep it there as whatever it contained was very poorly packed and finding a balance point was difficult. The weight was badly in need of redistribution, but Tomo knew better than to offer to do it now when Gran was in a hurry.

That completed, he next stepped inside the kitchen of the Bucket and retrieved another pack. This one wasn't nearly as heavy as the first one but was still a substantial weight. He strapped it to the donkey just behind its passenger and then took the reins of the mule. All this he did while trying his best to be quiet - Gran did have her walking staff in hand after all and could probably reach him for a good poke or worse. He led the animals directly away from the back of the tavern, heading for the closest edge of the cobblestones and the hopeful anonymity of the silent darkness. Once beyond the cobblestones in this direction only Fat Happ's farm lay between them and the forest and neither were worried that the village Reeve would stir from his bed to see who was passing by. Undoubtedly they would hear his legendary snores if they passed within sight of his simple home.

Tomo kept an eye on the trail but wondered at the old woman's orders. He didn't mind performing the often odd and menial tasks she gave him because he respected her, even loved her, and had since he was a small child. However, this time her demands were bizarre enough that questions were coming to mind and he had begun to worry that she was perhaps losing her mind. That wasn't so odd among people of her advanced age. Tomo's own grandfather had decided, at the age of fifty-seven, that he was a dead man, and refused to leave his bed claiming that it would be impolite to do so during his own wake. He hadn't lived but a few weeks after that and Tomo was sure that Gran was far older than his grandfather had been. And lately she had him doing some very peculiar things.

Beginning with the spring, his main occupation had been following a stranger around. A woman by the name of Jarma, or at least that was what she had told the officer in charge of Lord Ferule's garrison when he had confronted her. She claimed to be a prospector, a researcher from the university, and a hunter looking for a good place to trap during the next winter by turn. Gran didn't accept any of that and so Tomo had been tasked with following her. Odd of course but it was better than hoeing gardens or chopping wood for his wife.

Jarma had led him on a grand tour of the surrounding area and had proved more than capable of taking care of herself in the forest. In fact, she was a reasonably fine woodsman and took care to prevent anyone from following her. She hid her trail, doubled back often, and even wrapped the hooves of her horse in canvas sacks occasionally to further hide the tracks. Not that she seemed aware of his presence; rather she was just naturally cautious. Someone of even marginally less skill or poorer knowledge of the area than Tomo would have lost her or been caught several times over. In some ways, it had been exciting, because he knew just from watching her that she would have killed him without a thought if she had caught him.

Despite the danger it became almost like a game for Tomo and things had been going well. He followed the woman, she wandered the countryside, and Gran paid him for his labors. It sure beat farming. His hands were not made for the plow. Since a youngster Tomo had spent most of his days hunting and tracking poachers on the various estates of Lord Ferule. That was his element; his talent. Now he watched and then reported to Gran everything he saw Jarma do as the spring passed and summer came on hot and heavy.

But then things had changed with Gran. She started mumbling a lot more after he reported and was quicker with the switch than normal. Jarma had begun moving farther and farther out from Cobble and the other towns and this obviously agitated the old woman. When she started moving up into the mountains, Jarma apparently crossed some invisible line and Gran came to some sort of decision. She told Tomo that he need not follow the stranger anymore and to forget that he ever had.

And that wasn't the only odd things Gran had him do. Twice the stranger sent letters by way of Lord Ferule's post riders and it had been Tomo's duty to waylay the messenger and steal the letters back. That was beyond odd; that was criminal! The first time had been sort of a game for Tomo. He knew the post rider quite well so the challenge of slipping into the man's camp and stealing the letter from his pack without being caught had sounded like a fun game. It turned out to be even more fun, and quite a bit easier, than he had imagined. Chancing upon the man along the trail, getting the man drunk and then helping himself to the letter had not been quite so dramatic but very effective. The fellow hadn't suspected a thing.

The second time he had to pursue a letter the opportunity didn't present itself to accomplish the job with stealth and Tomo thought it would be too suspicious to 'accidentally' meet the fellow with a jug of homebrew again. Tomo had to disguise himself and do the job road-agent style, though he was thankful when the man hadn't tried to put up a struggle even when Tomo had taken the man's money pouch to make it look like a robbery. He also had to take the entire letter pouch and then abandon it in the forest, to be found later, so no one would know that the mail had been the object of the crime. To further throw off any suspicious officials, Tomo also cut the pouch open and spread the letters around as if the thief had gotten angry that there was nothing of value in the pouch. Finally, he had to hide for three days in the forest before returning home to ensure that any pursuers had been thrown off. The mysterious hold-up on the trail had been a major source of gossip ever since, but Tomo had never once been suspected.

Now that Gran was acting more strangely than ever, Tomo wished that he had read the letters before giving them to her. He wished that he knew how to read. His only recourse had been to ask Gran and that hadn't ended well.

"None of your business!" she had screeched, following it with a stout thump on his instep with her walking staff.

She had let him keep the money he stole from the courier after she exchanged them for other coins. It had only been a few coppers. They came in handy when he went home. His wife had stopped in mid-rant when she saw them. Profitable the trip might have been, exciting also, but Tomo had felt bad about the robbery.

Now he was sneaking Gran out of town in the dead of night. "No one can see," she said. "No one can know". Tomo wondered who had been Gran's errand boy before he moved to Cobble. Likely her son, Borel, or young Albrim her grandson.

Once they passed Happ's farm the way became rougher, though they no longer had to worry about being quiet. The trail Tomo chose was narrow with brush and branches blocking their way. The mule bulled through without complaint but the donkey kept shying away from something. Tomo wasn't sure, but thought that the branches sliding off the mule's backside might be striking the little animal in the face. Gran kept it on the path by sheer force of stubborn will. The poor donkey didn't have a chance in that regard. The mule wouldn't have either.

As the sun began to warm the horizon, Tomo turned off the trail and led the animals up a hill, their destination a small meadow at the top. Gran had specified exactly what type of location she needed and this matched it in Tomo's best judgment. The grass there was deep with plenty of soil, not barren and windswept like many of the lower slopes where floods and earthquakes had washed away the dirt. Just after dawn they arrived and Tomo helped Gran down from the saddle.

"Build me a small fire, Tomo," Gran had ordered, removing a folding shovel from the smaller pack on the donkey. "Make sure it won't be seen."

Tomo complied, scooping out an elbow deep hole in the loose dirt beneath a tree, using his belt knife to cut away the roots the flimsy shovel couldn't handle. Next, he built a small wall of loose stones on three sides to ensure the flames would be further concealed. The thick branches above should dissipate any smoke and he made sure to gather very dead wood to reduce even that. Satisfied with his efforts, Gran gave him a curt nod and began rooting through the many pockets of the cloak she wore.

"Now take your time and make a circle around this hill. Make sure that there is nobody around. I mean *nobody*," she said, shaking a bony finger beneath his nose.

Moving quietly into the forest, Tomo did what Gran told him. He was very thorough in his efforts; he was afraid not to be after the warning. Gran's tone of voice had convinced him that it would be better if they were not seen doing... whatever it was that they were here to do.

The forest was silent and still cool despite the heat that would be baking the world later in the day. Tomo studied every track and paused often to listen for sounds alien to his surroundings. Squirrels he found in plenty, but no sign of any intelligent life. Tomo was certain that whoever Gran might have been concerned about had not followed them.

By the time he returned, Gran had cooked them a meal of corn meal cakes and some type of unappetizing mush. Whatever else she might have done was concealed as she had repacked everything and doused the fire. She sat in the shade beneath the tree while the animals grazed on the deep grass nearby. Tomo noticed that the donkey was several feet away from the mule, a very odd occurrence as the little animal nearly always stayed right by its larger friend's side.

There must be water here as the summer sun had yet to bleach the grass into the same dusty brown as in the lowlands. Tomo added that bit of knowledge to his store and squatted down to eat his portion of the meal. Gran was chewing on a bit of straw as she watched Tomo eat, her eyes distant and contemplative.

Once he finished, Gran asked his help regaining her feet. Once she was up, she efficiently cleaned the cooking pot and repacked it, then stepped over to where the mule stood and untied the rope that held the big pack in place. With a thud, the pack slid off the mule, and the animal shied from the sound. The donkey moved even further away.

"Help me onto the donkey," Gran ordered, meeting Tomo by the smaller animal.

After lifting her into place, Tomo turned to retrieve the smaller pack, tying it once again onto the back of the donkey. He stood by, waiting for her next command, unsure what it was that they were doing or what he should be doing now. Gran smiled down at the waiting woodsman.

"Tomo, you're a good boy. You always were, even as a lad. I appreciate all you've done for me over the years, and what you've done for Albrim. Take this for your family," she said, handing over a heavy belt pouch.

Tomo took the pouch, marveling at the weight. By the sound, he knew it was coins, maybe more money than he had ever seen in his life.

"It's not much, just a few coppers, but it should see your family fed for a winter or two, even if you don't turn your hand at any honest work. Not that you ever have," Gran sniffed, always ready with a lecture but wearing a faint smile for Tomo that somewhat eased his guilt.

"Thank you, Gran, but I don't understand," Tomo said. Gran seemed... different somehow; less assertive, less attentive. Tomo couldn't remember ever seeing Gran look so distracted.

"I'm leaving, Tomo. I have somewhere I need to be. I've been here too long already, like as not. You'll need to do one more thing for me, and then you'll be shut of me forever."

Tomo was near to tears. "Gran, I don't understand, why are you leaving?"

Gran cupped the man's face in her gnarled old hand. "If I stay I'll be having a meeting with the headsman, Tomo. Lord Ferule won't stand for murder."

The blood ran from Tomo's face. "Murder, Gran?"

"Yes, murder. Someone will notice the woman is missing eventually and they'll come looking for her. They'll find nothing but stories of a suspicious old woman who watched everything the stranger did and even had her followed." Gran waved away Tomo's protests. "People see things, Tomo. Even as good as you are at hiding a trail in the forest, you can't avoid people seeing you leave town."

"But Gran, I haven't murdered anyone!"

"No Tomo, you haven't, but I have."

"Murdered who, Gran?" Tomo asked weakly, even though he was sure he knew who she meant.

"Jarma," Gran said, as calmly as if she spoke of the weather.

Tomo was shocked. "But Gran, murder?"

Gran waved his protests away. "She was getting too close to Albrim. Too near to finding him or that other Were that's out there somewhere. As long as she stayed in close I let it go, but someone talked, Tomo. Someone told her of our little outing when we took Albrim into the woods. Someone thought our little play was odd and Jarma found out. Her last letter proved it to me," she finished, pulling a much-folded piece of parchment from her pocket.

"What did you... I mean, how did you..." Tomo asked, his voice trailing away.

Her single lower tooth proudly on display, Gran replied, "With poison, Tomo. I ran the only tavern in Cobble. She had to come there eventually if she wanted a taste of ale and believe me, Tomo, she liked her ale!"

His mind racing Tomo blurted, "Gran if you killed her we only need to hide the body; there's no reason for you to leave."

Gran laughed. "Haven't you been listening to me? I've read her letters, and I know for a fact that at least one she sent made it through."

Naturally, Tomo protested that statement.

"Oh, it's not your fault Tomo, she surprised me on that one, and I didn't find out about it in time to put you on it. She suspected me and even named me to her superiors, I'm sure. Any decent investigator will come straight to me when they come looking for her. They might come in a month, maybe not for a year. Hiding the body will delay them, but that's only the beginning."

"Named you to who, Gran? Lord Ferule?"

"Best you don't know that, Tomo. Just remember that it's someone who wishes ill to Albrim and me, and that's enough."

Gran grimaced. "Sooner or later, they'll be coming for me and whether or not they find me, they'll eventually find Albrim, like as not, so I need to find him and get us out of this country."

"But Gran, where will you go?"

"Wherever, far from here, I suppose. It's best you don't know anyway. Being old makes for slow traveling so I'll need whatever head start I can get, like as not."

Gran smiled once more. "Be well, Tomo, and don't forget that one last task I asked of you."

She turned her donkey and rode away, making it halfway across the clearing before Tomo realized that he didn't know what the final task was.

"Gran, what's the final task?" he called.

Stopping the donkey she turned about and cackled as only Gran could. She pointed at the folding shovel where it leaned against the bole of a tree, and the big pack where it lay beside the still-grazing mule.

"Why, to bury Jarma, boy! And bury her deep!"

Chapter Seven

Dirk was accomplished at reading the emotions of others; particularly those with the power of life and death over him. The Duke of Firth was more than mildly annoyed and Dirk hoped it was not directed at himself. He was well aware that the messengers of bad news often bore the brunt of the displeasure in the initial reaction.

As the duke stood and paced around the underground chamber Dirk waited patiently, to all outward appearances anyway. He stood in the exact spot he had given his last report and did his best not to move an iota. Experience with nobility told him that here, where the other man had absolute control, you did nothing to anger him or bring his attention to you before he had dealt with whatever internal debate he struggled with. Explanations or excuses would only serve to anger him further.

With nothing else constructive to do Dirk studied the meeting chamber; seeing nothing he had not already memorized. The room was small and everything in it was covered in a thick layer of dust Dirk knew was painstakingly replaced after each meeting, although he didn't know exactly how. Whatever the original purpose of these rooms the duke or one of his predecessors had ordered them abandoned at some point and now they were used only for the clandestine meetings between Duke Lionel and himself, so far as Dirk knew.

Studying the duke told Dirk nothing new either; the man was who he was and revealed little in the way of emotions on his face. Today the duke had red hair, as it had been colored to reflect the latest style. He was covered from head to toe by a long blue robe of satin with the Firth crest embroidered on the left breast. The robe's purpose was to keep the dust away from the duke's clothing and prevent spies from suspecting where the duke had been. Firth's ancestral castle was kept immaculately clean, or as close as a building made of stone and mortar could be, and seeing dust upon the Lord's clothing could not help but draw attention. Dirk wondered how the man protected his footwear from the same dust.

"The slide cost us how many days?" the duke finally asked.

"At least three weeks, My Lord. A half-dozen workmen were lost and the roadbed buried beneath a dozen feet of rock. The engineers suspect a fault in the stone face."

"Is there nothing we can do to hurry them up?" the duke snarled.

"No, My Lord, your engineers say that there is nothing we can do but clear the debris before continuing on with the road," Dirk explained, careful to place the blame for the negative response squarely on the engineers and not himself. "Naturally they asked for more laborers, and I have done my best to comply."

"The prisons are getting empty are they?" the duke smiled ruefully. Healthy people kidnapped off the streets would be noticed but prisoners taken to the dungeons were often not seen again for years, if ever, and provided the cash-strapped duke with cheap labor.

"Very, My Lord, but I have... encouraged... your constables to be more diligent in their arrests. Word is that many merchants are pleased with your tough stance against crime of late, and your popularity in that quarter has never been higher."

This news brought a smile to the duke's face along with another bout of pacing.

"What of the tunnel? Is it complete?"

"No My Lord, but it remains on schedule. The engineers on the project claim that they should break through within the week; and the foundations for the bridge they begin next have already been laid."

"What other news have you?" the duke asked, changing the subject abruptly.

Dirk was ready. "Our agent in Aldragal has not been heard from in some months. This was the last missive we received from her. You indicated that I should wait until she had missed a third contact before dispatching another agent."

"Have you done so?"

"No, My Lord, I have further news to report that may alter your decision."

"You have confirmation that the agent is dead?" the Duke demanded, the original flash of anger seemed to have passed and now he was beginning to ponder the possibilities.

"No, we are not entirely certain, My Lord," Dirk responded before adding a gentle reminder. "But she has missed three consecutive reports."

Taking a moment to contemplate, the Duke continued to pace around the tiny room. Dirk waited patiently, shuffling several sheets of parchment on the table in preparation for the continuation of his report.

After several laps around the table, the Duke spoke, "According to her last report, our agent believed that a woman hid her grandson after the Were attack on her village. The agent believed the boy did not die as reported. We've seen that before in Were attacks. Foolish peasants never want to believe that their own family members will turn on them," the Duke laughed.

"Indeed, Your Grace."

"Her contact?"

"Her contact is a merchant named Pailin; a purveyor of furs who travels the road between Aldrigal and Skallist. When he failed to hear from the agent he detoured through the area in question and found no word of her, at least not directly."

"And the area is?"

Dirk took a step forward, stopping at the table and the map spread atop it. "Here, Your Grace, in a small village named 'Cobble'. It was the same place that your original agent was killed last year."

"Ah yes, that fool. He deserved to die if a handful of ignorant peasants found a way to kill him."

"I certainly agree, My Lord, but his death did put your plans in a precarious position. If I may remind you, the first agent was supposed to scout the area and use his wolves to convince some of the less hardy settlers to return to Aldragal, lessening the chance of anyone surviving to warn the city of your approach."

"And now there are even more settlers in the area as well as a small garrison. Plus rumors of a Were."

"Correct, Your Grace. General Handrick pulled all the wolves and Quargs back from the settled areas as you ordered and began scouting a more southerly attack route for his forces."

"It'll be harder to surprise them by not using the most direct route but thanks to that fool of a Were we have no choice now," Lionel growled, punching a finger at the offending map. The easiest and most direct route between Firth and Aldragal lay right where the new villages had been built. The duke might almost believe that the peasants had been settled there to watch for his invasion but all knew that it was impossible for an army to cross the Kenebruks. Lionel, himself, had once believed it.

"Tell me of the missing agent," the duke demanded.

"Agent Jarma has been a member of your Brakahl for ten years. Her cover story was that she was a Were-hating adventurer looking for signs of an outbreak after the attack on the village last year. Initial reports from Jarma indicate that her cover story was a poor choice as some of the survivors of the attacks saw her presence as disbelief that they had, indeed, killed the Were, and she met some resistance in Cobble. Therefore she changed her story slightly for nearby villages as she began her scouting sweeps."

"Looking for any signs of Quargs or our people?" the duke asked.

"Yes, My Lord, or anyone living deep within the forest that might have noticed something that they should not have."

"So who killed her? And why?"

"Agent Jarma's initial reports did reach us, Your Grace, but they are filled with little facts. A few of the more prominent citizens are named; the various Reeves of the villages, a handful of former soldiers and the like, but only one person was mentioned as being openly hostile to her. This woman is the only person named in the reports that might possibly have a motive for killing our agent, but I find it difficult to believe that she was the one responsible."

"Why?"

"Because of her age, My Lord. The lady in question is referred to by practically everyone in the various villages as 'Gran' and while that might be a reference to her as a grandmother it seems possible that it is her name is well. It could be that she is simply so much older than everyone else that no one knew her before she was a grandmother, and so her name has been forgotten. In any event she is the oldest person anyone in the villages know and is by Jarma's own report quite frail. It is difficult to believe that she might have killed our agent, though she might have the influence to order it done."

"What are her motivations?"

"As I reported previously, Your Grace, this Gran is the woman who's grandson was bitten by your Were agent last year. The boy reportedly died and the body was burned but Jarma could find no direct witnesses to the latter event. If the grandmother is hiding the boy she may have believed that Jarma was close to discovering him, and so had our agent killed.

"Foolish peasants. Eventually the boy will escape and begin killing people, likely including his grandmother, and draw even more attention to the area to our detriment," Lionel complained.

Dirk merely nodded.

"Well what is this new information you had that delayed my command? Cannot a member of the Brakahl be dispatched to search for our agent and this 'Gran' woman?"

"Yes, My Lord, but Lord Burstis returned yesterday, and I thought perhaps that you would prefer to send him rather than a simple Brakahl agent."

Lionel smiled. Dirk was a good man to have on hand. "Lord Burstis is back, you say? Fine, that is fine. I assume he completed his task?"

"Most certainly, Your Grace," Dirk replied. "It seems that the youngest Prince of Carstoth has gone missing. The lad will eventually turn up in the local slums when his newly acquired Curse drives him to kill his abductors and begin a rampage."

Lionel laughed. "A nice little diversion for Carstoth. Imagine, a Prince of the Realm Cursed and devouring poor peasants."

Dirk laughed on cue but saw little mirth in the subject. He wasn't against killing, he had cut more than one throat in his life, but felt uncomfortable using Weres. Why not just kill the boy and be done with it? Intentionally giving someone the Curse bothered him.

"And you believe that we should send Burstis rather than a normal Brakahl agent?" the duke asked.

"Yes, Your Grace," Dirk replied, ever ready with his notes laying atop one side of the map. "Burstis will have the best chance of surviving whoever is killing your agents."

"But one Were has died there already. Why would Burstis be better equipped in that regard?"

"As you know, My Lord, Burstis is the eldest of your... recruits... and has most fully acclimated to the Curse and his new lifestyle. Even if he was suspected as a contemporary of Jarma's it will likely be assumed that he is as human as she was, and therefore as easily killed. That will give him an enormous advantage."

Nodding his acceptance of the plan the duke sat on the dusty cushion of the dusty chair and fought to restrain the sneeze at the cloud his actions created.

"Burstis and Handrick hate one another, do they not?"

Dirk smiled ruefully. "They most certainly do, My Lord, but unless Burstis tarries overlong he should be away before Handrick enters the area. In truth all of your Were retainers hate Burstis as it was he that Cursed most of them. I will warn him to avoid other Weres at all cost; that should suffice to keep them from one another's throats."

"Fine, dispatch Burstis immediately to this village... Cobble was it? Have him search for word on the previous two agents to ensure that both were indeed killed and then find out who did it. Have him extract whatever knowledge this Gran woman has and kill her too. Tell him that under no circumstances is his Curse to become public knowledge. In fact, if he hears anything about a local Were he is to kill whoever spoke of it as well. If he finds any Weres, they'll likely be feral or too far gone to recruit, but tell him to use his judgment in that regard for we shouldn't ignore any potential allies. Be certain that he is aware that we cannot have any more attention being paid to that village than there already has been and by all means warn him to hurry; Handrick will have to attack soon or the mercenaries will desert for lack of payment. "

"Yes, My Lord," Dirk replied, shuffling his notes to the next page.

Chapter Eight

The Green Quarter of Aldrigal City was neither green nor a full quarter. It was actually more of an area within a larger section called the Market. Within the Market, all manner of herds and food products were brought into the city. The businesses there were those dedicated to providing the vast quantities of food the city needed each day.

Butcher Alley might be a name that brought fear to the minds of those unaware of the name's origins. A wide street now rather than the alley it had once been, it was the street where all the city's butchers were required by Royal Mandate to keep their businesses. Buildings along Butcher Alley were widely spaced and long pens to hold livestock awaiting slaughter lay between. Rivers of blood literally filled the gutters there as the daily slaughter of chickens, sheep, goats, and cows were processed for consumption. The new arrival to Aldrigal knew that she needed to travel along that street in order to reach her destination in the Green Quarter, and chose the late afternoon to do so. That gave the morning's bloodbath time to dry so at least you weren't forced to walk through the still clotting blood. Unfortunately it did nothing to dampen the smell. It was not her first visit to Aldrigal.

Gran allowed her donkey to make its own way through the pedestrians wandering along Butcher Alley. Those in service to the nobility had already made their daily purchases, taking the best of what was available for their masters. Rich merchants and city officials had been next, gleaning what remained. Next were the businesses that served food as part of their daily commerce. This time of day, the shoppers were the rest of the population, primarily the freemen and minor business owners. Those of lesser status could not afford fresh meat but would be out around dark to seek what remainders might be left. Bargains could sometimes be had if one knew where to look.

Just ahead, Gran could see the last of the butcher establishments and beyond that the edge of the Green Quarter. In the distant past, when the Green Quarter had been on the edge of the city, the area had been set aside so that those who worshiped nature had a place to meet and build their temples. Eventually those religions fell out of favor with the Lords of Aldrigal and most were abandoned or shunted outside of the city. This disdain for the druidic orders came to a head when Farmiticus the Fifth, the thirteenth Monarch of Aldrigal, found that his new young wife had more than a passing interest in a certain nature devotee. Farmiticus then made the decree that placed all the city's butchers along the main route to

the Green Quarter as a deliberate insult to those faiths, most of whose
followers were vegetarians. In the century since that decree, no one had
seen fit to reverse the edict and so the Green Quarter had languished to its
present state. Those who lived in other areas of the city were glad of that.

Not that Gran cared one bit for the difficulties of those who lived in the
Green Quarter. The fools could have left long ago if they had wanted to.
Who ever heard of a wilderness religion with temples in a city? No real
religions, that was for sure. All Gran needed to do was find one person;
someone she had known long ago.

A group of children moped by her, hands in pockets or thrust inside
their clothing when pockets were in short supply. Either they had nothing
at all to do, or were planning some sort of mischief. Gran suspected the
later. They stared at the stranger riding on the donkey, cautious of anyone
riding such an animal. They had seen donkeys before, of course. The less
reputable butchers occasionally slaughtered old specimens when supplies of
mutton or beef ran low. Those who couldn't afford any better didn't bother
to complain; they were happy to get meat at all.

Gran pointed her walking staff at one of the urchins. "You, lass. Where
is the Temple of the Endless Fields?" she demanded. She thought that she
remembered, but didn't want to spend hours wandering about if her
memory failed her. That did occasionally happen, regardless of what she
told others.

Starting at being addressed, the children scattered, the little girl
chosen by the pointing staff the only one to hold her ground. Gran always
could judge a child.

"Left at the next cross street, and then right again. You can't miss it.
It's got a tree growing through the roof!" She said. This little girl had lived
her entire life on Butcher's Alley and in the Green Quarter. It was the only
tree that she had ever seen.

Gran thanked the little girl and tossed her a coin, then used her staff to
beat away the children that tried to take it from her guide. Using her
donkey as a roadblock she gave the girl a head start to escape her 'friends'
before continuing on her journey. She ignored the sullen looks of the larger
children who had seen the copper coin as their own just due.

"They'll grow into rabble and worse, like as not," she mumbled to
herself.

Following the girl's directions brought Gran directly to the temple she
had wanted. She was reasonably sure that she hadn't needed the directions
but remained glad that she had asked. Everything she passed had looked
unfamiliar; many of the buildings were gone or so changed as to be
unrecognizable. The temple looked the same, if a little more rundown than
she remembered. But then again, she had been here only twice before. The
great tree still rose above the courtyard wall; ready to bear its crop of nuts
when again the seasons were right. What a ridiculous place for a sacred
tree.

She didn't bother to get off her donkey, instead reaching out and
pounding against the gate with her walking staff. She wasn't certain that
she could return to the saddle if she got down. She had sat astride the little
beast for many hours this day and her knees were stiff and painful. After a
few moments she knocked again with no more results than she had the first

time. Waiting was not something that Gran preferred. She could be as patient as a tree in the winter; waiting for the spring to grow again, if she had good reason. This was not one of those times.

Turning the donkey about, she whispered into its ear, grasping its mane in both hands for better purchase. Obediently the little animal kicked out, forcefully opening the gate so that it slammed against the wall behind it. Just within the portal, a small man dressed in the manner of a monk stood open-mouthed in surprise. The gate had very nearly struck him.

"Well don't just stand there," Gran snorted, guiding her donkey through the now open gate. "Fetch me to Haran immediately."

Chapter Nine

A chandelier of pure crystal refracted the light of the flames off the reflectors in such a way that the room seemed to shimmer with tiny, flickering diamonds that swayed with each errant breeze to give the whole effect an undersea-like quality. The diners ignored the shimmers; they had been here many times before and the chandelier's effects were old news to them. A relic of an older, more affluent time, Duke Lionel von Firth had in recent days considered selling it, along with many other things of value he had inherited. Several old tapestries and paintings had already found their way to collectors in other lands.

"My Lord please send my regrets to your lovely bride. To be ill and miss such a wonderful meal is quite a tragedy," lisped the rotund merchant sitting to the Duke's left. The man was a pig and had on two occasions attempted to show his affection to the Duchess through drunken passes. Fortunately for him he was quite rich, and well worth keeping alive for the time being. Trade with the coast was more important for Firth than it had ever been and the taxes and bribes this one man provided were among the most lucrative income sources the duke had remaining.

"Yes, my dear wife has been feeling poorly of late; we hope it is the precursor of good news," the Duke replied, smiling his practiced smile. She had been feeling poorly of late but her absence from this dinner had more to do with avoiding the merchant than anything else.

"Is she with child?" asked Baroness Ezdrella von Firth from her seat of honor to his right. Until he could provide an heir, she was it, and so her interest in the subject was keen. From her voice and mannerisms, you couldn't even tell that she was filled with spite at the thought.

"That has not been determined, Ezdrella. Lady Ralina has been ill of a morning often of late, and her physician has said that it is too early yet to tell."

"Oh what wonderful news," she lied. "Finally you'll have the heir we've all prayed for."

"It is not yet for certain."

"No but I just have a good feeling about it; we women are sensitive to such things. And such a blessing the child will be after the misfortune you've had with your previous wives. How many has it been? Four now?"

Lionel smiled at his cousin. Two could play the false sincerity game. "Five, Ezdrella. I've had as many wives as you've had children."

Her eyes flickered slightly at his words. She despised having children and it had taken her and her husband seven tries to have five children survive and it wasn't until the last one that they managed a child that didn't have her husband's cleft palate. She would never allow a child with such a disability to be her heir. Another husband should have been chosen for her but the Baron Lagash was a powerful man when her father arranged it. She daily gave thanks to all the powers that he was finally dead.

"Yes, well I have been blessed with fertility. There are so many who truly want children and yet never have any," she said, actually producing a blush to accent her words. Then her face turned aghast as she added. "But I'm certain that you are not to blame for your lack of an heir, dear cousin." Her voice held that perfect quality of surprise and regret that made her words seem a slip of the tongue to anyone unfamiliar with her or the art of the genteel insult.

Lionel continued to smile, waving away the 'accidental' insult with one hand. "I remain confident that one day I will provide our nation with an heir; perhaps even more than one. My Lady Ralina is young and strong and we have been married little more than a year."

Ezdrella nodded her thanks at his overlooking her faux pas but inwardly clapped with glee. None of her cousin's wives had ever shown the slightest sign of being pregnant and she didn't believe for one moment that the latest one was either. Four women in just over fifteen years had held the title of Duchess; each dying of some mysterious accident or disease once she failed to become pregnant. Ezdrella stood ready to see to it that if her sterile cousin ever did provide an heir, it would never see the day of its birth.

Whatever rejoinder his cousin had in mind, Lionel was spared suffering through it when a page approached his chair and bowed low over the small silver platter he carried. Upon it a carefully folded note lay awaiting the duke's attention.

"Excuse me, cousin," he said, taking the note. It said what he hoped that it would and regretfully he begged his companion's leave.

"It is a small matter, but one I need attend straight away," he told Ezdrella, asking her to take his place as the host for the remainder of the meal. Everyone at the table stood politely as he left; many making disappointed noises at his leaving but in truth no one cared save for those planning on asking for some type of favor.

The page led the way through the corridors, leading the duke away from the smell of roasted mutton and mince pie to the small sitting room off his bedroom. Lionel swept through the door to find a disheveled Adermon, the engineer still dusty from the road. The man stood to his feet, a half-eaten supper on the table before him.

"Sit my friend, finish your meal," Lionel said, grasping the man's hand quickly before waving him back to his chair. "You've obviously just arrived; you must be famished."

"Indeed, My Lord, it is a pleasure to eat a hot meal for a change," the man said, resuming his seat but not reaching for his knife. The food could wait.

After ordering the page to bring them some wine, Lionel chose a thickly upholstered chair near the fireplace before speaking again.

"And what of our little project."

Adermon shook his head ruefully. "My Lord, you should have brought me in sooner; a great deal of time and effort was wasted that could have been avoided."

"I apologize, old friend. I believed it beneath you to supervise a simple tunnel and besides; you had plenty to do in searching for the gold deposits we so desperately need. That was the greater priority," the duke explained, actually speaking some truth. His chief engineer had been busy looking for the gold but it was secrecy that had forced the duke into bringing in an outside engineer for the road project. Adermon was too much of a public figure and his disappearing into the mountains for weeks or months at a time would have been too obvious to conceal.

"I understand, Your Grace, but the engineer you brought in was just a lad! Barely out of the university."

"He was highly recommended," the duke replied, then thinking to himself just how cheaply the man had come. Every copper had to be pinched these days.

"And for good reason; the lad is very bright, very gifted, but he has no practical experience and for an engineer, that is crucial. Books can tell you a great deal, Your Grace, but the actual doing teaches much more."

"Duly noted, old friend. Never again will I even consider such a thing, no matter how trivial, without first consulting with you about it. So you now have the project back on track?"

Nodding Adermon stood up, taking up one of several large scrolls from the floor beside him and bringing it to the duke. Unrolling it as he walked, Adermon placed it on another table and used the candlesticks and knickknacks already there as weights to hold it open.

"The lad had drifted off his target; only by three degrees, but that was why the tunnel opened up here," Adermon explained, pointing to a point on the topographical map that indicated a steep cliff face, "rather than here," he finished, pointing to a gentler slope a short distance away. "I have fixed the direction and started a second crew on the other end. When I left there two days ago they had less than two fron of rock preventing them from connecting the two."

Lionel leaned forward to see. The tightly spaced lines that crisscrossed the map told him very little although Adermon had endeavored to teach him the rudiments of it. The problem was that since the map was of a mountainous area the lines were so thick in places that they became nothing more than a jumbled mess to Lionel. But, that was why he paid Adermon so well, or at least he had when the mines still worked.

Pleased the duke leaned forward all the more, as if the details of the map would be even clearer to him if he were only a little closer. A fron was about the length of his own body. "So they may very well be through even now? Wonderful news, my friend!"

"Yes, My Lord, they should be, in fact. With the addition of my own men to the, ah, workers you already had on the project," the engineer began, he had no use for the prisoners the duke had been using to that point, "I have a third crew under the direct command of our engineering student clearing the rock slide from the road here," he again pointed. "And the bridge across this ravine was finished the day I left."

Lionel wanted to leap with joy but kept his reserve. Adermon had almost put them back on schedule. "Then what do we lack in finishing the project?"

"There is still work to be done, but we are largely finished. A bridge needs to be built across this ravine; and another across this river. With the completion of the tunnel and the rockslide cleared, I can focus all our resources on the bridges and have them completed in perhaps a month, sooner if the rock on the walls of the ravine are suitable for use as footers as they seem to be at first glance. Otherwise we need only clear a path through the forest," he said, trailing a finger across the map following the track that had already been scouted across the most level ground, "a task your prisoner labor force will excel at, and the road will be finished."

"Amazing, so this will be done before winter hits?"

Adermon wavered. "Before it strikes the lowlands, yes My Lord, but not in the mountains themselves. Of course, the tunnel will keep us from having to climb to the upper elevations, so the cold weather will not be a real hindrance."

"Fine, Adermon, just fine," the duke said, standing now and clasping the engineer on the shoulder. The timing could hardly be better. "I should have came to you first, I truly apologize. Please, sit back down and finish your meal. When the wine arrives, drink it all. I'll have someone prepare you a room here tonight; you deserve a night of relaxation," Lionel said before clasping the man's hand again and leaving him.

Blushing under the praise, the engineer nodded his head but did not sit again until his liege had left the room.

Resisting the urge to kick his heels together, Lionel crossed the few steps to his personal chambers almost in a run. Excitement was threatening to burst from him; what would his servants think if their duke were to let out a whoop of glee? Once behind the door he allowed himself a long moment of self-satisfied joy before calming himself. The success of the road was good news, but not the last detail that could go wrong. It was time now to concentrate on the other phases of his plan.

Moving a tapestry aside Lionel opened the small door and removed a thick sheaf of parchments from their hidden alcove. He sat with them and began to page through carefully; looking over facts and figures long memorized but still as fascinating to him as ever. It could work! It would work! It had to work, otherwise Firth would become a minor territory of a larger neighbor. And he would also be dead or worse; living on the run or as a prisoner in some dank dungeon. Neither were acceptable; he would take the long shot and gamble to either secure his and Firth's future or die.

Chapter Ten

Seeing no reason why she should have to walk when she had a perfectly good donkey to ride, Gran refused several offers to dismount, choosing rather to ride the beast to the door of the temple itself. There, it was the narrowness of the door that convinced her to step down, rather than any thought of desecration. This particular order believed in thin, narrow doors. Gran couldn't exactly remember why. More foolishness, like as not, but she wasn't surprised to see it.

Once off the donkey, Gran used her walking staff to drive the young monk ahead of her, jabbing him unmercifully whenever he hesitated. She was here to see Haran, and see him she would!

The temple was bare and dirty, but then again, it had always been dirty. The sect of druids that served here felt that to remove dirt and dust was an insult to nature and so accumulated debris was generally left wherever it lay. Small pale weeds and blue-leaved ivy had sprouted in the corners where passersby did not trample them underfoot and the room was dark from the grimy windows.

"Your temple is filthy," Gran berated the monk, quickly silencing his prepared explanation with a well-placed jab of her staff.

"Where's your worshipers? Where's the people who are supposed to come here to pray?" She demanded, again poking the man whenever he attempted to answer or even slow his pace.

"You have no worshipers, that's why! Who wants to worship in a filthy temple? To pray kneeling among rotting vegetation, like as not! You've taken a few tenets and exaggerated them beyond comprehension, you fool."

The monk didn't bother slowing, nor demanding to know how he was at fault for religious dogma developed before he was born. He was learning fast how to deal with Gran. He kept his protests to himself and walked fast. The care of the sacred tree was important for reasons this frightening old woman could not hope to understand. At least, that was what he had been taught.

As a focal point of the temple, a stone replica of the sacred tree from the courtyard had been constructed. Why anyone needed a statue of something that lived a stone's throw away was another absurdity that did not fail to come to Gran's attention. The poor monk paid dearly for that one in both verbal and physical ways. Behind the statue another narrow doorway earned Gran's ire as she had to turn sideways in order to squeeze through. Beyond it was a set of dusty stairs clean only down the exact center, from the trailing robes of the few monks that still lived here.

Huffing like a bellows from the climb, Gran briefly considered ordering the monk to carry her up the remaining stairs, but didn't want to give the young man the satisfaction of knowing she couldn't make it on her own. Grumbling replaced her barbed insults as she was forced to conserve both her breath and her energy. Sixty-two steps later (Gran had counted them), the stairs ended and a small hallway led back over the main shrine.

Here it wasn't only the doorways that were narrow but the hallway itself. At the stairs, it was wide enough for two people to pass abreast but as it continued, it narrowed drastically until it ended no wider than the narrow doorway there.

"More foolishness," Gran stated, only then regaining her breath. Turning sideways so she could keep her walking staff in the hand nearest the monk in case further prodding became necessary, she squeezed into the room with a last blistering curse.

Gran found herself in a much larger room dominated by a massive bed that must have been assembled on the spot. Two large windows overlooked the tree in the courtyard and the bed itself was angled so that the occupant could see the tree. The corners of this room shared the filthiness of the lower floor but most of the furnishings appeared to be well maintained. In the room with her were two other monks besides the one that had guided her and in the bed itself a small, wizened old man who almost disappeared among the gleaming white pillows and comforters that were piled around him.

The two monks began berating the younger monk for bringing an outsider into this most special chamber, but Gran would have none of that, dropping her walking staff and stalking to the bedside so that she could peer in at the ancient shell of a man that lay there while also interposing herself between the monks in order to end the argument.

"The Grand Vizier is not receiving visitors today, old one," began a female monk of middle years. She had a massive wart on one cheek. Gran ignored her at first but then the monk made the mistake of taking the older woman's elbow in preparation of leading her away. Before her fingers even found purchase, the monk felt the sting of Gran's switch.

"I came to talk to Haran. Is this him?" Gran asked, leaning over to peer at the man in the bed.

"Yes, dear lady, this is Haran," said another monk; stepping to Gran's side and motioning for her to keep her voice down. "Grand Vizier Haran is resting and really should not be disturbed."

Gran leaned over to look at the pale white form lying among the white sheets and pillows. "What did you do to him?" she asked, her voice somewhat faint with surprise.

The second monk laughed. "We have done nothing to him, old one. We have merely cared for him, to make his final days as comfortable as possible. No more than he deserves for a century of service to our Sect."

It was not apparent if Gran was listening to the woman or not. She seemed fixated on the old man, staring into his face as if trying to see something not readily visible to the others.

"Haran?" she asked softly. "Haran, is that you?"

The old man started slightly and his eyelids began to flutter. First one eye, then the other cracked open and he peered out from the prison of his flesh. Unable to move his body, his weak arms only twitched and one leg straightened as he gazed out at the holy tree. Smiling, he whispered a name.

"Here, Grand Vizier," said one of the monks. "Have you a need?"

"Water," he whispered.

Lifting a pitcher of cool water, the monk poured a drink for the old man, lifting his head to prevent choking. Content, the old man relaxed back against his pillows and again closed his eyes. Believing that he had once again fallen asleep, the three monks readied themselves to throw Gran out of the room, bodily if necessary, so that the leader of their order could rest.

"I had the most wonderful dream," the old man said, his voice still weak, but stronger after the drink.

Dutifully the youngest and only male monk, the one that had guided Gran to the room, picked up a sheet of parchment and placed it against a portable writing board. He dipped his quill pen into ink and waited expectantly to record the old man's prophetic dream.

"It was from my youth. Someone that I knew," he whispered. "I heard her voice calling to me. 'Haran', she called. I haven't heard anyone call me by my name in decades." The old man smiled.

"Who was it, Grand Vizier?" asked the nearest monk, likely the eldest after the Grand Vizier.

Gran studied this monk, seeing in her a true strength of will and purpose most people she encountered did not have. Her hair was as gray as the old man's, but she remained young enough to care for him. Gran would guess her at sixty or so and knew that Haran, the old man, was likely well past ninety by now. It amazed her to realize that. She truly had lost track of the passing of time.

"It was a woman, a wonderful woman. She taught me so much, yet we only knew one another a short time. Her name was..." his eyes grew vacant as he groped for the name. "... Gran... Yes, that was it! Gran! It was short for something else... I cannot remember..."

"That's because I warned you then if you ever told anyone what Gran stood for, I'd switch you," stated Gran firmly, pushing past the monk and taking the old man's hand in both of her own. "Even now you remember that warning, like as not."

For the first time since awakening, the old man's eyes truly focused on something. Staring hard up into Gran's face, his face broke out in a smile.

"Gran, it really is you," he whispered, tears gathering. "I thought you were long dead! I should have known better."

"That's right, you should have. A problem you always had, Haran," Gran replied, the softness of her voice dulling the sharpness of her words. Tears were beginning to well within her own eyes.

Smiling so broadly it looked as if his deeply wrinkled skin might break, Haran hung on every word.

"I have missed you, Gran. You should not have left."

Gran smiled back "It was necessary, Haran. Life leads us where it will and uses no paths of our own choosing."

"A quote from the holy book of Durod. Ever the scholar, eh Gran?"

Excited to see their leader so alert, the eldest monk tried to interrupt.

"Grand Vizier! If I may, there are certain orders of business we must discuss. If you would like to ask your... friend... to come back later, I am sure that we could arrange a meal for her, and the two of you could spend some time becoming reacquainted."

Looking up at the sixty-year old monk, Haran only saw the youth she had once been. "Adema, I shall spend this time with my friend. The business can wait or you can handle it yourself. I am past the point of care over the worldly concerns of our order. Now leave us, all of you."

Face blazing red from the rebuke, Adema ushered the other monks from the chamber, all but slamming the narrow door closed behind her.

"She's a hot head," laughed Gran, dragging a step stool over so that she could climb up and sit on the edge of the massive bed.

"She is highly dedicated to our order, but also very ambitious. She has waited many years for my death so that she can take my place. She has been dutiful in my care, but begins to fear that I shall outlive even her," Haran sighed. "I am past the point where I wish to continue living. She can have the order; I wish to return to the soil from which we all spring."

Gran placed her hand on his shoulder and was shocked at how tiny and frail his bones were. She remembered Haran as a young man, hale, strong, and full of life.

"You'll go soon enough, like as not, so do what you can while you are still here," she admonished.

Haran smiled up at his old friend. "And what would that be, Gran? I can no longer rise from my bed nor even feed myself. I have nothing left to offer this world."

Gran plumped some pillows and stacked them behind her back. She needed the support after several days in the saddle.

"Your mind is still clear. You have a great deal of wisdom and knowledge there that the world can ill afford to lose."

Haran closed his eyes a long moment, perhaps thinking back to his childhood. "My mind is not always as clear as now. Knowledge remains, though I do not always have access to it. But wisdom... ah Gran. Wisdom is your strength, not mine. And much of what I know, you know also. Perhaps even more."

Grimacing she replied. "My knowledge cannot compare to yours, not in certain areas. You were always the smart one, even if you were devoid of common sense at times."

Haran laughed again. It was weak but Gran was glad to hear it. 'Those who would give up on life must first give up laughter.' Another of the useless quotes her mind was cluttered with.

Studying her face again, Haran suddenly looked surprised. "You are in remarkably good health, Gran. Far better than I, by the looks of you."

"My work is not done and so I must tarry on," she said, smiling at yet another quote from the past. She was surprised at how many she was recalling today. It must be the influence of seeing someone from so long ago.

"Yes," Haran said, but he looked troubled.

They sat and shared old tales for some time, each embarrassing the other by turn with some of their memories. Both decided that the other had retained only those memories that made the other look foolish.

"I cannot believe you remember that, or that I did it to begin with!" Gran cackled at one point.

Haran smiled, his face sore from such unaccustomed mirth. "But you did, Gran, and with bells tied around both ankles."

Silence fell as each chuckled over the story. Haran was beginning to tire, so Gran reluctantly changed the subject.

"Haran, I didn't come here just so you could embarrass me with my past indiscretions," she began.

He struggled to raise one hand enough to wave away her explanation. "I understand, Gran. I'm just thankful that you came at all. I haven't felt this alive in years. It must be the influence of sitting with such a beautiful woman."

Despite herself, Gran felt a flush crawl up her cheeks. Haran had always been a flatterer.

"I need information, Haran. Something I can't quite remember but it may be within your experience."

"Anything, Gran. If I can help you, I will," he said earnestly.

"I know that, Haran. You always were a good lad."

"It's been a long time since anyone called me a lad, Gran. I appreciate that."

Gran reached into an inner pocket of her shawl and pulled out a piece of folded parchment. "This came to me a few months ago. It means a great deal to someone I care about, but I cannot identify it. I thought perhaps you could help."

She smoothed the parchment flat and held it up for him to see. Realizing that the light from the window was making it all but transparent, she picked up the writing board the young monk had left on a table. She attached the parchment to the board by use of the spring-loaded clip at one end and brought it again to Haran.

Gran studied it again as Haran looked it over. It was a drawing Gran herself had made of the medallion worn by the Were that had killed Borel. She had sent a copy of the drawing with Albrim. Many times in the last year she had locked herself in her room and looked at it, trying to decipher the odd symbols and the tree insignia. Not for the first time Gran wished that she had the original medallion with her, but Sir Garen had taken that to his father. She was simply glad to have had enough time to replicate it on this parchment.

The rear of the medallion had been smooth, but the front had been filled with intricate carving. A tree in full bloom dominated the center. Around that was a circle that enclosed it, separating the tree from the symbols. Gran had decided that two of the symbols were Dwarvish and another was Elvish. At least they resembled letters of those languages that she was somewhat familiar with. Nothing else about them gave her the least bit of information, and that frustrated her to no end.

Haran peered at the page, squinting and then pulling his head back as far as he was able against the resistance of the pillow. Gran moved the board a little farther away until her friend indicated that he could see it better. He looked at the page, moving his lips as if translating the symbols, which made her hopeful. Her arm was beginning to shake from the effort of holding up the board when Haran finally whispered that he had completed his examination.

Gran returned the parchment to her pocket, carefully folding it to prevent the drawing from getting smeared. Haran was lost in thought, or perhaps his mind had wandered; either way, he appeared to be searching his memory for something. She decided to wait for him to speak rather than risk diverting him from his line of thinking.

"I believe I have something for you," he whispered.

Gran eased forward, squeezing his upper arm in thanks as she waited for his next words.

"Your eyes are still so bright," Haran said, then abruptly changed back to the subject at hand. Something in those bright eyes must have convinced him to stick to business for the moment.

"The symbol of the tree is one I recognize, of course, because it looks much like ours," he explained, looking meaningfully at a grime-stained banner hanging on one wall. "The symbols are a mystery to me, save for one that is in the written form of an ancient Elven language. That symbol means 'branch', but that isn't very helpful. As you know, the tree is a very common symbol and I can think of at least five other groups or nations who share it with us."

"Or more, like as not," Gran agreed.

"Yes, like as not," Haran smiled. "The organizations that I recall using a tree such as this include two groups of my fellow Druids and one from a group of rangers. The nation of Evergreen may or may not still exist; it lies well to the north of Aldrigal and there has been a lot of unrest in that area over the years. It was a minor kingdom even in my youth and very well may have disappeared by this time. The last use of this symbol I know of is for the library of Istipol. I know nothing of it but have read that it used a tree to represent itself."

Gran was startled at the mention of the library, but hid it quickly. Patting the pocket that contained the drawing, Gran replied, "The library of Istipol is long destroyed; at least that is what I heard in my own youth. It lay in what is now the merchant quarter of Aldrigal but was razed to build some nobleman a new outhouse, like as not. The buildings built atop it are now ancient in their own right. I am reasonably sure that the kingdom of Evergreen has fallen as well. Also I can think of no reason why any of those groups would have anything to do with the person I obtained this from."

"Who would that be?" Haran asked. "The person you obtained that drawing from. Perhaps knowing that will trigger my memory."

Thinking hard before replying, Gran considered just how much to divulge to Haran. Finally, she decided that the poor old dear likely wouldn't remember it very long anyway, and there was no one that she trusted more. She decided to share it all.

Gran spoke and time passed. Eventually Haran's caregivers came in to feed him and reluctantly provided for Gran as well. The youngest monk, the one Gran had prodded with her walking staff, seemed to resent her presence the least and reported that he had cared for her donkey. In between these few interruptions, Gran told the story of the Were attack and the devastating losses the town of Cobble had suffered. She also told of

Albrim and his fate. It was the first time she had spoken of that night in such detail, without holding anything back. By the time the sun began to go down, she had cried more than she cared to remember.

Haran slept more than once, but somehow managed to absorb the main points of her story. He was amazed that such a thing could happen in this day and age. He, like Gran, remembered the Were War that had cleansed Aldrigal of the evil beasts so many years ago. At least, it was believed by most people that the Weres had been eliminated. Obviously they had survived. Above all, he reassured Gran that everything she had done was for the best. Gran didn't believe him; she felt certain that Haran would never have allowed a Were to go free, even if it was a relative, but it felt good to be agreed with.

"So anyway, I copied the medallion as near as I could before I gave it to Sir Garen. I made two copies and put one in Albrim's pack when I sent him away," she sniffled.

"And you do not believe the attack by the Were was random?"

"No," Gran scoffed. "It was too well planned. The wolves were brought in to draw the militia away on a wolfing. Then once they had been lured well away, a smaller village was destroyed to lure Sir Garen, the only person in the area with a weapon capable of killing the Were into an attack where he was wounded. Next, the Were and all the wolves descended on Cobble in one coordinated attack. Random! The sun rising in the morning is more random, like as not."

"So what would a Were want with a town like Cobble? Was there anything of value there?"

"Not likely. Nothing in that town was worth anything. The town was only a couple of years old and there were no merchants or nobles living there. In fact, the only thing Cobble had that separated it from a dozen other towns was our cobblestone square."

"Cobblestones are of little value to a Were," Haran joked.

"Perhaps it wasn't something in the town the Were was after, but rather someone," Gran mused.

"Perhaps," Haran agreed. "You knew the people of Cobble. Who among them may have had enemies?"

As bazaar as the idea was, Gran still gave it some serious thought. Everyone who had lived in Cobble had been born on estates belonging to Lord Ferule. She had delivered most of them herself. Only K'jord had been an outlander and he had died before the Were breached the tavern window. If he had been the target of the attack, the Were would likely have left then, unless it decided to remove all the witnesses, which was also a possibility.

Gran rejected that idea. K'jord had been a farmer, nothing more. He had confessed to Gran that he had run away from a bad marriage, nothing more than that. It would take more than a runaway husband to draw the wrath of a Were.

The only person of any real importance in the town had been Sir Garen, but he had only been there when the Reeve of Spicer had requested help from Lord Ferule with the eradication of the man-killing wolves.

"I can think of no one, Haran. The people of Cobble were peasants or at best, freemen such as my son Borel. He was a bowyer. We also had a cobbler, a blacksmith, and a tanner. No one who had ever been more than a week's travel from Cobble or an estate of Lord Ferule's in their lives."

They shared a few moments of silence, finally broken by Haran.

"It is a mystery. Perhaps the answer is the most obvious one. A Were wanted to kill or just take revenge on society. The medallion may have been nothing but a pretty bauble taken from one of his victims."

"I'm going to need more information."

"Yes," Haran said. "I'm sorry I was not more help."

Gran kissed him on the forehead. "You were more help than you can ever know, even if you didn't help me with the medallion," she said, wincing at her lie. He had been a great deal of help to her, forcing her to do what she had suspected would be necessary when she came here.

Haran smiled even as he again drifted off to sleep.

When next the Grand Vizier awoke, he found that his old friend was gone. The hour was late but the light of one of the moons lit his room just enough to see that someone sat in the chair by his bed.

"Gran?" he asked.

"No, Grand Vizier. It is I, Adema. The old woman has been gone for several hours now. She told me to tell you goodbye and safe journey."

Haran sighed. "I shall never see her again, Adema. Growing old is a part of nature, a part of renewal, as we both know, but there are times when it is also very sad."

Adema said nothing for some time, only rocking slightly in her chair. "You knew her from when you were young?"

"Oh yes, I was a boy really. Perhaps ten. I met her when I attended the university. Long before I joined our order. I found her fascinating. We spent a great deal of time together during those years. She came here to visit me once or twice and then she just disappeared until today."

"She also attended the university? Surely not in the same classes. As a matter of fact, I find it hard to believe that she was there when you were. Could you perhaps be mistaken, Grand Vizier? There must be more than ten years difference in your ages."

Haran laughed aloud. "Oh yes, Adema. There is more than ten years difference in our ages."

Adema was confused. "You were ten when you met at university and yet she is more than ten years younger than you?"

His head almost felt strong enough to lift off the pillow. "Stars above, no! Gran was one of my instructors!"

Chapter Eleven

Entering the Merchant's Quarter this late in the evening was simply not going to happen. That area of the city had long ago been completely taken over by mansions of tremendous size, including those of most of the well-to-do of Aldrigal. Only the richest of the merchants could afford to own a home there now. They had been pushed out long ago by nobles with more money. Over time the entire area had been surrounded by high walls and even watchtowers in some places. No better defended area was there in the city, short of the Royal Palace, and those who could afford to live there had no problem contributing to the upkeep of the mercenaries employed to keep the Quarter safe - mercenaries who were not about to allow Gran and her donkey access to the richest section of town after dark.

Servants by the thousands were needed to maintain the fine mansions and serve the rich people who dwelt there. Such people lived close to the Merchant's Quarter by necessity and were generally honest, hard-working people. However, as in many large cities, the wealth of one area drew the worst elements of the rest of the society. In and among the small businesses and simple homes that filled the streets around the Quarter were a number of cut-throats and petty burglars that preyed upon their servant neighbors in order to survive as they planned for that one great theft that would feed them for the rest of their lives.

Attempts at theft in the Merchant's Quarter were dealt with harshly. The city watch rarely interfered with the punishment given by the mercenaries. Most believed that it was fitting justice for thieves and such. Besides, with the mercenaries in the employ of the richest and most powerful members of the city, including virtually all of the ruling class, there was little anyone could do to stop it anyway. Rarely did a week go by that at least one corpse without a head or hands was found hanging from the Gem Street Gate. Not that this form of justice served to reduce the number of the thieves in the area. It seemed that there were always more willing to move to the city or simply out of the poorer slums elsewhere in Aldrigal and take the place of those who died.

A donkey was not a daily sight in the streets near the Merchant's Quarter and Gran was drawing a great deal of attention. Some people along her route were trying to decide just how much they could get for the animal and where exactly they might be able to sell it. Being Gran, she had a pretty good idea who was thinking larcenous thoughts as she passed them and so shared her most direct stare and contempt as needed.

"Been too long since I've been here," she said softly to her donkey. "Everyone I knew is long dead, like as not. Perhaps I should have stayed in the Green Quarter until morning."

The donkey didn't reply. Gran guided him along as the darkness fell. Somewhere near here was a tavern, or at least one had existed once. At one time, it was a safe place for travelers to stay, free from the dangers of the poorer elements of the area. She hoped it was still there. If she failed to find it or some similar place of protection, she would be unlikely to keep her donkey or her few coins. She might even lose her life as well.

Gran sniffed. "As if riff-raff like these would dare lay a hand on us," she told the donkey, knowing even as she said it that an area like this would have a number of people who would do just that.

Just as darkness truly began to fall, Gran caught sight of a familiar sign.

The buildings on this street were a uniform two levels in height and shared their walls with their neighbors. Each was narrow and made of mud brick with a single narrow door and one window directly above it. When last Gran was here, the buildings had been painted bright colors and banners had flown from the rooftops. Now they were unpainted and dull with many broken shutters on the windows. Ahead to her left, the homes suddenly ended and in their place was a wall of wooden planks. Looming over the wall was a larger building set back from the street. In the midst of the wall was a simple open gate and it was above this that she saw the sign of the Jackdog.

A fantastical beast that appeared in many local legends, the creature depicted on the sign combined elements of the jackrabbit, known for its wisdom and speed, as well as the dog, known for its fierce loyalty and nobility in Aldrigalian fables. The Jackdog combined those elements into a single mythical beast that in many stories saved humanity from one tragedy after another. The Jackdog had been adopted as the name of this inn two centuries before, and Gran had once been a regular visitor. That had been long ago. On the sign was a faded Jackdog holding a dagger in its mouth. This referred to an ancient Aldrigalian fable where the Jackdog saved the city of Aldrigal by using a dagger to reflect sunlight into the eyes of a giant. So faded was the sign that the shiny blade Gran remembered was little more than a grayish blur.

She rode her donkey into the gate just as two burly men were preparing to bolt it for the night. They welcomed her warmly and one of the men led her beast away as the other completed the closing of the gate. Then she was politely led across the courtyard and into the door of the old building. Above that door was a newer sign showing a Jackdog at rest in a field of clover. This sign was based upon another Aldrigalian fable, where the Jackdog saved the city by luring a fantastical marauding beast into falling asleep in a field, thus diverting it from its destructive tendencies.

Accepting the young man's arm, Gran allowed him to help her up the steps and through the door. Within she saw little that she remembered.

When last she had entered the Jackdog, the front doors had opened into the large common room where the various guests and customers of the inn could gather together to eat and drink, perhaps even listen to a bard.

Now, the front door opened into a smaller room that was dominated by a large chest-high desk that covered the whole of the farthest wall. To the right and left were doorways with the scent of some sort of stew and fresh bread drifting delightfully from the right. That was the direction of the kitchens, so at least that had not changed. To the left came the clink of mugs and a few laughs. Apparently, the present proprietors felt that a smaller common room would not harm their business.

Her guide sat her pack down beside the door, pointed her towards the tall desk and then went back out into the night. Gran made her way across the room, her walking staff tapping its way across the polished wood floor. The furnishings of the Jackdog were in no way rich, leaning mostly towards local hardwoods, but were clean and well kept.

Gran found herself glad to be there, and not only because of the danger in the streets she had just left. She felt safe here and could feel the tension knots in her muscles relaxing more and more even as she penetrated further into the building. Likely some type of magic was involved. Make the customers feel relaxed and they would be more likely to spend money as well as being more likely to return. Gran didn't mind that. If they made a little more money by use of the spell, then so be it. In her mind the customers were paying for the relaxed atmosphere as much as the food and beds.

The tallest human Gran had ever seen stood behind the desk. The man was as thin as the poles Gran used to support her bean vines with a shock of unruly red hair that waved back and forth above his head and a bright smile among the hundreds of freckles that swarmed his face.

"Welcome, dear lady. Welcome to the Jackdog," he said warmly, his deceptively deep voice booming about the entrance room. "Are you looking for a room for the night or a meal? Perhaps a drink to drive away the night's chill?"

Gran sniffed. "A chill, on a summer night? Just like a man, to try and invent such a foolish reason to drink!"

Laughing, the man leaned on the desk, still towering over her. "A room and meal, then? You're not a local, so you'll certainly be staying the night?"

Nodding, Gran agreed that she would be. "I will stay the night, and something to eat would do well. I'll also need the answer to a question or two, if the proprietor is here."

The smile did not fade in the slightest. "I am that proprietor, my lady. Why don't we have your pack taken to your room and then get you something to eat? I'll be along to join you there and you can ask me anything that you want."

"Fair enough," Gran said, watching as a young man picked up her pack and disappeared in the direction of the common room. A young lady, with hair the same color as the tall man, came into the room and motioned for Gran to follow her. Just as she was about to pass through the doorway, Gran turned back to the tall man and crooked a finger at him. He seemed not to notice but Gran was sure that he had. It was only fair that Gran warn him.

Through the door lay another room; this one small with yet another open door across from it and a wide stairway to their right that traveled up to the second floor. The wood of the steps and the floor was covered by a carpet of linen and Gran followed the girl's lead by scrapping her shoes clean on it before descending the two steps to enter the common room. It looked nothing like she remembered, either. It was not smaller than she recalled, as the back wall had been removed to extend the space in that direction. The clamor of the kitchens also came from that direction, so Gran suspected that this lower floor was one continuous circle. Why that had been done, she didn't know but cared less.

Following the girl, Gran was led through the scattered tables and past a long bar where a dozen men were drinking. The tables held only a few other customers. Gran suspected that most locals went home before dark and those still here were spending the night. Only two were eating, which was no more than Gran expected. Trust a man to prefer strong drink to good food. And based on the delightful smells, it was good food.

To her mild surprise, Gran was not shown to a table in the common room, but rather taken beyond them, to a wall covered completely by curtains. With a pull on a grass rope, one section of curtain slid back to reveal a small alcove with a table and two chairs. A private booth.

"How nice, child," Gran said, moving to take a chair for herself. Once seated, she was surprised to see the girl still with her, obviously waiting for something.

"Fetch me some food, girl," Gran said. "I'm very hungry."

"Of course, my lady. What will you have?"

It took Gran a little aback by the question. It had been decades since she had been offered a choice of meals in any inn or tavern. Not that she had frequented very many. They were too expensive for commoners to indulge in often. She thought hard for a moment. What was it she had eaten the last time she was here? Then it came to her: the perfect meal.

"Do you have any souse?" she asked.

"Yes of course, my lady. It's been a specialty here for many years. I shall bring it directly out," she replied, offering both a smile and a curtsy to her customer before drawing the curtain.

Gran sat quietly, using the time to ponder the little that she had learned from Haran. Druids and rangers were not likely to be supportive of a Were, particularly one that did so little to control his bloodlust as the one that had attacked Cobble. The kingdom of Evergreen was long destroyed; the last king died without choosing an heir from among his six children causing a civil war. They had seen to the deaths of one other quite well, along with all the grandchildren. The line had died and the kingdom had been absorbed by its neighbors. Gran didn't precisely remember the events but was familiar with the story.

However, the library of Istipol, that was something else entirely. She had not been completely honest with Haran. She knew more of it than she had revealed.

Istipol had once been a sage of great wisdom and a favorite of the king of Aldrigal many decades ago. She had also been a collector of the written word, and by the time she settled in Aldrigal had accumulated a number of books. Such things were rare and many of those Istipol gathered were ancient. Some she made copies of and others, it was said, were hidden away. Her own research filled a dozen large volumes and these also were added to those in her personal library. A library that once stood not so distant from where Gran now sat awaiting her meal.

Such a story as that of Istipol was not rare. It seemed to Gran that history was filled with such events. Someone of rare foresight, and yes insight, would seek to gather together knowledge for its own sake and then someone else would follow them and destroy or disperse it. So many times the knowledge was used to subjugate or conquer someone else. Libraries, so rare and magnificent in this day and time, simply attracted trouble. Istipol had proven that.

The trouble began when Istipol herself died. During her life, she had been too powerful, too well connected, for trouble to overcome her. She was a talented politician and remained on the good side of three different kings of Aldrigal. Unfortunately, her influence died with her.

Not immediately, perhaps, but soon enough. Gran had read of the quarreling that had begun among her apprentices before their former mistress was even cold in her grave. When a wizard from afar heard of Istipol's death, he had raided her library for certain magical texts he wished to obtain. The quarreling apprentices had stood no chance at stopping him, as none would cooperate or work with their fellows. The most valuable texts had been taken.

The surviving apprentices had taken what was left and departed, leaving a single servant as the only person dwelling in the grand library. When the next king of Aldrigal desired a new palace to be built for his mistress, he chose the site of the library, and so it was razed. Only the foundation stones were left. Well, the foundation stones and the servant. Somehow, she had managed to remain there, now working in the new palace. That woman had been Gran's grandmother.

A formidable woman, as Gran well knew, despite having only known her a very short time. She had lived long enough to have a single child, a son, who in turn married and produced Gran. Then her father had left, abandoning his wife and daughter. Eventually he turned up again, but with a new family. A family that consisted of a wife and two sons. Sons with red hair.

The curtain was swept back to reveal the tall man from the front desk carrying a tray containing a large ceramic dish that steamed delightfully. Gran smiled as the tray was placed before her and the top of the dish removed, revealing the souse she had asked for spread thickly atop both halves of an entire loaf of fresh bread. To either side sat small wooden bowls. One contained string beans and the other a sliced tomato. Also on the tray was a pewter mug of cool milk. Tucking a linen napkin into the collar of her dress, Gran began eating even before the tall man closed the curtains and sat in the other chair.

How she loved her souse! And this was an extraordinarily flavorful recipe. It had belonged to her grandmother and was made from the finest cuts of hog meat; namely that which was boiled from the head. Among the nobility, these were considered to be almost waste products. To those born to the lower classes, the head was among the best, most flavorful cuts of meat they were likely to get. Gran had grown fond of it over the years. The souse of the Jackdog had always been better than that she cooked herself.

"I enjoy seeing someone enjoying our food," smiled the red-haired man. "My wife will be pleased to know."

Gran didn't speak, just glared at the man as she ate. When she had eaten all that she could, which didn't come close to half of what had been brought, she sat back and sipped from the mug of milk. It was very cold. The cellars of the Jackdog were cool all the year round, Gran knew.

"You Tadric's boy or Peron's"

Smiling, the man sipped from his own mug; Gran suspected it was something stronger than milk.

"I'm not sure if I've just been insulted or not," he laughed. "In fact, I am the son of neither. However, I am the great-grandson of Tadric."

"Great-grandson?" Gran nearly shrieked. Again, she had forgotten how long it had been since she was last here.

"That is so. You know, my lady, it has been many years since I last saw this signal," he said, making the identical motion Gran had made earlier. "When I was a small boy people would occasionally show it to my father, but not often. Perhaps once or twice per year. These days it simply does not happen. I thought that all of those who knew of it and its significance were long dead." He took another sip before continuing. "I am pleased to be wrong."

He didn't look pleased, Gran noticed. Not upset, exactly, but perhaps a combination of surprise and curiosity. She studied him closely as she sipped her milk. He seemed like a good enough lad.

"Once that signal meant something," she explained. "I assumed that the sons, and yes even the great-grandsons, of Tadric or Peron might remember."

Nodding once he replied, "We do remember. I am here, am I not? The owner of the Jackdog rarely delivers customer's meals himself. My family carries a long memory and my father shared with me the knowledge of who we are and where we came from. He also told me of this sign," he crooked his finger again, "and what it represents."

Placing his mug on the table the man continued. "But now I would like to know who you are and how you know of it."

Gran noticed and approved that the man had not stated the request as a question. He might be thin as a pond reed, but this lad had iron in his spine. It just might be that this fellow truly did understand what they were talking about. He might not be the type of fool that Gran was used to dealing with, after all. Not that Gran would ever assume that of anyone.

"I will explain all, but first, I would have your name."

Seeing no reason to deny her something she could obtain by speaking with anyone that lived nearby, the man hesitated only a moment before replying.

"My name is Kelendle. I am the current owner of the Jackdog."

Gran shrugged as if the name meant nothing to her, but in reality, it meant a great deal. It was the name of her father's second wife's father. Likely, it had become a name used and reused within the family. She was satisfied that Kelendle was who he said that he was. She had already been satisfied just from his appearance, but she had always been one to make doubly sure when possible.

"This is not my first visit to the Jackdog. I came here often in my younger days," she tapped the uneaten souse. "I was having this souse when your grandfather had yet to make an appearance in this world. I've been away for some time and come here out of need."

Kelendle looked somewhat skeptical, but not entirely so. He used a finger and thumb to rub between his eyes.

"And your name is?" he finally asked. This time it had been a question.

"My name is Gran. I am your blood kin though it is quite thin by this point," she sniffed. "In truth, I do not claim kinship with you, boy, but I do claim the right of this," Gran finished, once again crooking her finger in the appropriate sign. "Long ago an agreement was made between me and mine to honor this."

Leaning back in his chair, Kelendle almost lifted his mug again, but thought better of the idea and instead pushed it away. Keeping his mind clear was a good thing in Gran's opinion. He needed to be careful with this whole situation.

"Tell me what the symbol means. Tell me its origins," he said. "I will judge the story you tell against that one told to me by my father. Your answer will determine whether or not I believe you and honor the request."

Gran nodded once, sharply. The boy was not asking anything untoward. Settling herself more comfortably she told a tale that she hadn't shared in many years.

"There came a time when a servant of Istipol found herself alone in the world. Her mistress had died and she had managed to find a position within the palace built atop her former employer's library. She knew certain things that no other knew but kept them to herself. Unwilling, she was, to share with anyone something her mistress had warned her not to divulge."

After taking another sip of milk, Gran continued.

"She eventually married and in her late middling years she had a son. She told her secret to that son who later abandoned his first wife and fled the city. Returning many years later, with a new wife and sons, he bought this inn and became a successful businessman. Ashamed of what he had done, he contacted his former family to find that his first wife had died and their only child, a daughter, was teaching at a university."

Kelendle interrupted. "The version I have heard differs slightly to this point but not substantially so. I was told that the first wife was an evil harpy of a woman who drove him away with her spite. Please continue."

Gran sniffed. "You can take it from me that she was not a perfect woman, but she and her child deserved better than abandonment."

He nodded his acceptance of the statement, so Gran returned to her tale.

"In time, the guilt of the father drove him to accept monastic vows, and his years spent as a warrior convinced his superiors in the church to promote him to a position as a Church Knight, or paladin. Before his death, he extracted a vow from all of his surviving children to honor this sign," she again made the motion, "and to vow that their descendants would do the same. He then shared the secrets of his mother with his sons, but not his daughter," she sniffed; still upset over the slight after all these years.

"A vow to help one another, whatever the need, and to protect one another. This was his way of looking after his children, even though he chose to leave all of his worldly possessions to but one of those sons."

"In the last years of his life, he saw grandsons who had turned to thievery and could not bear to see them jailed or killed. A vow we have always kept," Kelendle added. "Even when distant cousins came through, fleeing from justice, we hid them. When men we knew were thieves and murderers gave us the sign, we hid them, gave them money and helped them escape the city."

"Just so," Gran agreed. "Although there was also the matter of the secrets of Istipol, which were in fact a significant part of the original vow. The man gave the secrets to his sons but he gave the right of usage of those secrets to his daughter. That portion of the vow is why I am here."

Kelendle looked very interested now. "Then you are a descendant of that daughter?"

Gran hesitated, but finally agreed. There was no sense in trying to convince Kelendle that she was that daughter. "Yes, so I am. From her, I have inherited the rights to the usage of the secrets. Just as the father had foreseen, in his one and only prophetic dream."

"A prophetic dream?" Kelendle asked. "This, I have never heard about."

"The dream was the basis for the old paladin's return," Gran explained, refusing to say her father's name. She had never really forgiven him for abandoning her and her mother. "In the dream, he saw that his blood would one day need something from the secrets of Istipol, but he also saw that revealing those secrets to the wrong people would bring great harm. He knew that only through his daughter's line could the secrets be used properly, and then only sparingly and at the proper time."

"Fascinating," Kelendle said. "Needless to say, I am convinced of your identity, my lady."

"Call me Gran, everyone does."

"Thank you, Gran. You can of course call me Kelendle, or 'cousin' if you prefer. If you will excuse me, I am going to have your belongings moved to a better room. Family deserves only my best," he said smiling.

Gran waved him back to his chair. "That's not necessary; I'm not used to the best of anything. Wherever my pack is now, just leave it there. I want to talk to you about the secrets of Istipol."

Kelendle did not sit back down, but did pause at the curtain before leaving. "You'll need to accept my word on this, Gran. You deserve the best room in the inn. That is, if you want access to the secrets."

This time Gran didn't try to prevent his leaving.

Chapter Twelve

She tried to avoid tapping her walking staff on the damp stones as her guide had asked, but she found it difficult to prevent on the uneven floor in the pitch dark. Mumbling under her breath, she continued to hold onto the belt of the young girl ahead of her, occasionally tugging on it to slow the youth down.

Gran was tired, but felt a building sense of excitement, as well. As a girl younger than the one whose belt she held onto, she had been told many stories of the great library of Istipol and the alleged secrets that remained hidden, even after the building itself had been razed. It had always irked her that her father, curse his faithless heart, had never shared the secret with her, only with her half-brothers. He had told her that it would be either her or her descendants who would utilize it but that she could not know the secret until the proper time. Fool men and their foolish prophetic dreams.

Kelendle had been true to his word. After a few hours of questioning to further convince himself of Gran's identity he had shown her a secret passage built into the wall of her room. Narrow to the extreme, the passage ran through the walls and under the Jackdog before opening into a tunnel that she believed ran straight under the wall into the Merchant's Quarter. The tunnel had ended at a ladder that apparently opened somewhere within the Quarter itself, but another secret door had been opened behind the ladder that gave them access to still yet another tunnel. This, Kelendle had assured her, led to the secret remnants of the library.

"Be silent and be cautious," Kelendle had told her. "We must not be found in the tunnel, or the authorities will take the Jackdog."

Gran was well aware of what the tunnel had been used for in the past. It looked far older than the Jackdog, but likely had been found and refurbished by thieves to use to enter the rich Merchants Quarter. Her father had undoubtedly known of it as well, and had taken steps to keep this section a secret, even from the thieves. That was why he had bought and built onto the Jackdog as he had. Gran had never even suspected that the tunnel existed.

Kelendle continued to lead them along the tunnel, nearly stooped over to avoid bashing his head on the low ceiling. His daughter Cora, short for a longer name she had assured Gran was 'horrible', was taking the trip for the first time as well. She was the same red-haired girl who had taken Gran's order for souse at dinner the night before. Her father was taking the opportunity to share the secret with Cora, keeping it alive for another generation.

Where had the tunnel originally opened? In someone's basement, or was it just another cave in the ground? It didn't smell like a sewer but then again, it could be an abandoned sewer. Although damp it had no standing water, which was a blessing. After what seemed to be an eternity of feeling their way along, Gran felt Cora stop ahead of her.

Cora whispered with her father and then somehow managed to switch places with him. A few more whispers preceded a loud clicking sound and suddenly a pale blue glow outlined a door ahead. Grateful for the light, Gran followed the others through an opening that formerly had looked like only a blank wall, and joined them in an alcove that was twice as wide as the tunnel they had just left. Pulling up against the walls, the father and daughter allowed Gran to slip past them to a black curtain that hung on what was otherwise an undecorated wall.

As Gran approached the curtain, she saw it move slightly from the breeze stirred by her movement. The blue light came from behind the curtain and showed through at the bottom and in one small place near the center. She looked back once at Kelendle, and received an encouraging nod, although it was obvious that they would be going no farther with her. She was to go through the curtain, but now she was on her own.

The curtain was black, and felt like silk. Gran could detect no spider webs or dirt on the curtain, at least not by feel. It opened down the middle and when she parted the two halves, a brilliantly bright blue glow burst from the next room. Squinting and stepping through, she heard Cora gasp at the light's beauty. Once she was through the doorway and hidden behind the curtain, the light went out and she was again in total darkness.

"Fool wizards," she griped, again feeling her way along in the darkness. She counted her steps and found another door after step number twenty-three. The doorknob felt like rusty iron, and protested loudly when she turned it. It did unlatch, though Gran had to pull mightily to force it open.

Stepping through into the darkness beyond, Gran was surprised by the faint glow that appeared once she was in the next room. It began very softly and then gradually brightened, saving Gran's old eyes from the sudden explosion of light she would have expected. She waited impatiently as the darkness fell away.

The source of the glow was not readily apparent, but Gran saw no shadows in the room, not even her own. No torches were visible; it was as if the room itself was lit by sunlight from directly overhead. The walls of the room were cut granite blocks and large enough to have required magic to place them. Above, the room rose to three times her height, and the walls fell away at least that far in each direction to her right and left. The far wall was probably as far away as either of the side walls, and all three of those were covered in shelves filled with books of all shapes and sizes. Behind her, the oak door was dominated by a branded symbol very similar to the one Gran had found on the medallion she had taken from the dead Were. Not exactly, but similar, and her hopes rose because of it.

Her heart picked up the pace of its beating as Gran observed the treasure trove of antique artifacts the shelves held. Books filled with anything other than someone's personal diary or journals were expensive things, and rare outside the homes of a few rich nobles. Gran had once

taught in a university that felt blessed to own seven. There had to be at
least sixty tomes here; and all of them once the property of Istipol. They
must be priceless!

But money was not Gran's purpose here. It had never been a priority to
her, and she wouldn't begin worrying about it now. She had come here
looking for some knowledge of the symbol on the medallion, driven by some
idea she had yet to fully form in her mind. Why did she believe that the
library would be of use? It was at least a century out of date. Something
had brought her here. There was something here that she was meant to
find, or to do. Perhaps something she was supposed to read. She hoped so.
Reading had always been a pleasure of Gran's and something she had not
been able to really indulge since she left the university.

Not sure where to begin, she walked to the left wall and reached for the
first book on the end. A faint crackle of energy and a light shock came from
the touch.

"Ach!" she screeched, far more offended than hurt. "So I am to be killed
with lightning? I was brought here just to die, like as not," she grumbled,
looking at the floor to see if she had passed across any carpet on the floor,
but seeing nothing there but pure white sandstone. Thinking that perhaps
it was now safe, Gran reached for the same book once more, and was again
rewarded with a minor zap of pain.

Growling, Gran stepped back from the shelf and thumped the book
once with the base of her walking staff. The wood trembled from the
coursing electricity that passed into it. Surprised and not a little frightened
at the power, Gran dropped her staff and stepped back further, wringing
her hands to ease the tingling.

"I understand you now," she grumbled, looking around the room for
some hidden guardian. "I'm not supposed to touch that book."

No one replied, so Gran tried the next book in line and was shocked
again. She moved up a shelf and then down one, receiving a shock each
time. Moving down to the far end of the original shelf, she again felt the
bite of a spark.

Throwing her head back, Gran shrieked her frustration and moved to
the bookcase on the back wall. She hesitated before touching a book there.
Would she receive the same type of shock, or possibly even a worse one?
Perhaps here she would be burned by a ball of fire. Was she missing
something? Had she forgotten something important? Kelendle had
mentioned nothing of this, but it was likely he didn't know. He and his
descendants had not been allowed to actually enter the library.

Stepping back Gran again studied the room, looking for any minor
details she might have missed before. Seeing nothing and having no better
ideas, she shifted her walking staff to her other hand so as to give her right
a break from the shocks. Stalking purposefully back to the shelves she had
just left, she touched a book covered in blue leather at random.

No shock this time. Relieved but also concerned, she next touched a
book on the third set of shelves and felt a solid bite to her index finger.
Shaking at the thought of being shocked again, she went back to the first
shelf and again came away shaking her finger in pain. Another touch on the
same 'safe' book as before did not hurt, so she tried the one next to it.
Nothing.

Feeling finally safe, she must be intended to look through only the books on this one shelf, Gran grabbed the blue book again, this time intending to pull it off the shelf. When she came to herself, she was sitting on the floor in front of the shelf, the ends of her hair smoking slightly.

Clambering back to her feet, Gran began a tirade that eventually included every curse she knew backed by a few that she made up on the spot. She denigrated the shelves and every book on them individually, while punctuating her words with numerous 'like as nots'. When she finally ran out of breath, she thought hard on what she had learned. Finally, she concluded that she needed more research.

Obviously she wasn't supposed to open that book, but just touching it had not shocked her. She tested it again, but was not shocked. It was only when trying to remove it that she had been struck by the magic. Testing books on the shelves above and below it, she again received the bite of the lightning, although after the jolt that had knocked her down they were nothing more than minor annoyances. The book she sought was on this shelf, she just had to find the right one. At least she hoped that was all it was. If there was some sort of password she was supposed to know, then Kelendle and his daughter would likely find her charred corpse here when finally they ventured through the curtain. If they could even pass the curtain, which was not a certainty.

Carefully Gran touched each and every book on the 'safe' shelf and received no more shocks. However, she discovered that touching one particular book with thin sheets of split pine for a cover gave her a tingle of a different sort; this one a cool shiver of anticipation that ran along her spine. Taking deep breaths to ease her anxiety; Gran chose that book and pulled it from the shelf...

Nothing happened! No shocks, no blackouts, nothing! Holding the heavy tome in her shaking hands, Gran nearly stumbled over the upholstered chair she found suddenly and conveniently behind her. The upholstery of the chair perfectly matched the color of the book's bindings, with an identical wood grain. She was grateful both for the opportunity to sit and to find that the chair did not also share the book's rough wood feel. In the back of her mind was the thought that the chair might have a greater meaning. It just might mean that she was to read the book here and only here. There would be no leaving the room with any of the ancient texts, not that she could try to do it and live anyway.

Sitting down with the book in her lap, Gran then noticed a faded blue ribbon protruding from between two of the pages. Cracking it open at exactly that point, Gran decided to begin her research there.

So far, so good. No detonations, as she had half expected. The book was open in her lap and she was still alive. The print appeared to be enormous, making it legible even to her old eyes.

The heading on each of the pages the ribbon had marked announced the title of the book as 'Istipol's Gift.' None of the entries were dated but there was a paragraph on the left-hand page that was underlined in brownish ink. Gran decided to begin her research there.

Now she had only to read.

Chapter Thirteen

Snow fell heavily on the highest slopes of the Kenebruks as winter
worked hard to bring an early season to the lands below. Here on the
western side of the mountains that had already resulted in a few morning
frosts. Scouts on the eastern side had reported an autumn warm spell that
was making for a bountiful harvest. All the better for the plans of the Duke
of Firth.

Stepping carefully around the piles of fresh wolf dung Lionel inspected
the troops gathered together for that purpose. The Firthians looked proud
despite their lack of uniforms. This was the man they were sworn to, and he
was here to personally visit with them. The mercenaries looked bored but
held to tight ranks because of the life of discipline they had led. They cared
nothing for the duke and were here only for the wealth they had been
promised but pride would not allow them to look less proficient than the
regular soldiers.

Lounging around behind the others, gathered together in somewhat
tribal groups were the Quargs; confused and bemused by the fuss being
made over this one man. Perhaps he was a great chief among the Firthians
but to stand without moving for hours on end while one strutting peacock
walked among you was more than they could comprehend. They were here
for the plunder, same as the mercenaries, and hoped that this might signal
their long-awaited attack beyond the mountains.

For their part the wolves ignored the whole proceedings. They hunted,
slept, came and went just as they always did. The smaller ones generally
paid attention to their Quarg masters while the larger gave deference only
to the Weres. Game in the area was all but non-existent and the wolves had
to either make do with the tame meat provided by the soldiers or roam far
into the lowlands looking for a kill; much to the consternation of those
living on the Firthian frontier. As a pack they knew that it was time to
move on to new hunting grounds but their masters would not let them. The
wolves thought, as much as animals think, that the Quargs and Weres were
being poor pack-leaders.

His inspection complete, a task the Duke of Firth found oddly
pleasurable, he exchanged salutes with Handrick and then returned to his
command tent, an angry General Nigel Intona dogging his heels.

As tents go it was somewhat spacious with four large rooms contained
within its walls. It was made of silk but had a thick raw wool exterior that
could be attached in bad weather and the recent nip in the air had provided
that. A long table had been built out of unfinished local timber and provided
an adequate place for Lionel to meet with his generals, provided one was

careful of splinters or tearing a valuable map. The floor was made up of several layers of canvas topped by a thick carpet of pelts. The sheer number gave some hint as to the state of the local game population.

Pouring himself some wine Lionel tried to hide his mirth from General Intona. The man was nearly beside himself with anger at being left out of the invasion plans until now. Not only could the man not be trusted to talk, he kept a number of mistresses at least two of which were spies known to the duke, he simply couldn't have handled the tensions that grew naturally between the various types of troops. Particularly in an encampment so far from civilization.

"Be still, Nigel. It was for the best and you know it," he finally said, pouring the man a drink as well. "You have done a marvelous job with the regulars and that was vital to keeping our enemies off-guard."

Only slightly mollified the general accepted the pewter mug but didn't drink; his anger went too deep for that.

"You are my liege and I obey your commands," he announced stiffly, not realizing that he looked ridiculous standing at attention with a pewter mug of wine clutched in one hand.

"Relax, old friend. You remain a part of Firth's plans and will continue to be. You must accept that sometimes it is best to do things outside the normal paths. Tell me the truth; would you enjoy being in command of wolves and Quargs?"

The general said nothing but looked thoughtful. If he was at all honest with himself he would have to realize that it was unlikely he could have handled such a command. Likely his pelt would have long ago joined those on the floor of the tent. For the first time in several days he visibly relaxed; if only slightly.

Each took a sip of their wine, a foul vintage likely home-pressed in some filthy commoner's hovel. Lionel couldn't help but think of some foul-smelling peasant crushing unripe and diseased grapes with their unwashed feet. Unable to get the thought from his mind he set his mug aside as those he awaited entered the tent.

Gathering around the table the various officers seemed unsure as to who should sit where. With the arrival of the Duke the hierarchy of the seating had changed enough to sow confusion. Lionel allowed them to find their own places and waited patiently. In the end he motioned General Intona to sit on his right and Handrick on his left and this seemed to help the others.

Beyond Intona sat the other human officers from Firth; to his left the various Weres deemed suitable for command. The humans watched the Weres closely as if they might suddenly give in to their Curse and attack. For their part the Weres, unconsciously or intentionally, kept broad smiles on their faces that revealed their obviously pointed incisors. They seemed to find the officers' discomfort quite amusing. Beyond both of these groups sat the most powerful of the various mercenary captains and the Quarg chieftains sitting on boxes, chests, or even upon the floor.

Rising, the Duke gave a short greeting and an explanation of why he had assembled them this day. Most remained ignorant of just who they were going to invade, most thought they were going to raid one of the richer border cities for the plunder, and Lionel had no intention of letting them in on the whole secret until everything was ready; the time would come when even the most stupid among them would realize where they were going.

Taking the time to be introduced to the various leaders, Lionel used his famous charm to the best of his abilities. The Quarg chieftains continued to be unimpressed since the duke had made no effort to impress them with his physical prowess and did nothing more than smile when they took turns lifting a heavy crate. Their people were eating better than they had in years and the promise of plunder still seemed likely so they accepted him for now. The mercenary captains were only mildly impressed; they had each known nobles from a half dozen nations and found one much like another; so long as they were paid the mercenaries would follow.

Once the pleasantries were complete, most of those gathered were allowed to leave, keeping only the core officers for a more thorough briefing. Handrick ensured that the tent was well guarded, and the guards were posted a discreet distance away to avoid eavesdropping, and then he also returned to take his seat. The duke began as soon as the Were was in place.

"Who has the map?" Lionel inquired. Dirk appeared as if by magic from one of the curtained-off rooms with an enormous sheet of parchment in his hands. Gently placing it on the table before his employer he stepped aside so the various officers could see, all of them half or completely rising so they could lean in as close as possible. To most of them it meant nothing but all found themselves inexplicably drawn to it.

"First things first," Lionel announced. "General Handrick, would you please give us a summary of your forces?"

"Certainly, My Lord," the Were said, standing up and placing his hands behind his back as if a child repeating a devotional. Everyone continued to be surprised at the deference the Were showed the duke, save for Lionel himself.

"The Quargs have continued to drag their feet but I have around twenty-five hundred of them gathered at present though their numbers wax and wane from time to time. They resist all attempts at training but are beginning to look better despite their best efforts." He paused to allow the gathered officers a moment of laughter.

"The Firth regulars stand at two thousand men, five hundred of which are cavalry and these are the best of our soldiers," he continued, nodding to General Intona. He wasn't exactly lying, the cavalry were the best of what he had, but he had been cautioned by the duke that the general needed to have his ruffled feathers smoothed. Despite his resentment the general responded, his chest swelling slightly at the compliment.

"The last of the mercenary companies have arrived giving us around fifteen hundred of the black hearts. All that have not yet arrived are the troops from Herth and Kelsten, who are due sometime after the harvest."

"Bah, Herthians are nothing more than barbarians," scoffed Colonel Nira. In command of supply for the army, she was the only female in the tent.

"Indeed, but they are utterly fearless in a fight," explained General Intona. "If you need a wall breached or a fortified position stormed, they're the perfect shock troops"

"And Herth has agreed to provide us with five hundred of them," added Lionel.

"Well Kelstenians are certainly not barbarians, but what help will they be?" demanded Colonel Barant, the commander of the Firthian cavalry. "Surely they cannot muster more than a hundred men in their whole miserable little nation."

Another laugh from the assembled officers had to die before Handrick could respond.

"They have actually promised us three hundred men, Barant, fifty of which are mounted knights in full armor and the rest bowmen. They will be of tremendous use, I assure you." No one protested his words; fully armored knights were a force to be reckoned with and other than the Quargs the army had no archery units, the duke having kept them in Firth to defend the duchy.

"And that, with the wolves, represent the entirety of our forces," finished Handrick, "save those sitting in this room." This was a veiled reference to those carrying the Curse. Although it was known to everyone here, it remained a point of unease for those without it.

"And this is enough to take Aldrigal?" asked a surprised Barant. The youngest in the tent, he was prone to speaking before he thought.

"Provided we have surprise, yes," replied Handrick. "I have been working for two years to design our assault and now, with the help of General Intona's helpful suggestions, we believe we have something that will work. General?"

The big Were took his seat again, smiling slyly to himself. He had more than soothed the General's feelings now by allowing him to explain the plan. Puffing up with importance Intona, who had learned about the plans only a few days before, picked up a stick and used it to point at various points on the map as he spoke.

"This is our forward encampment;" Intona began, pointing to a spot on the eastern slopes of the Kenebruks. "It has already being cleared by laborers provided by the duke," he smiled at Lionel, not mentioning that the men were merely the prisoners from his dungeons who had so far survived the brutal building of the road. "There we will gather our forces and launch a three-pronged attack on Aldrigal City. As you all know; if you take the city, you take Aldrigal."

"Yes but you're trying to take a city of eighty thousand with, what, eight thousand?" demanded another officer. Lionel couldn't remember the fellows name but knew he was in command of the spearmen.

"Eight thousand plus the wolves," Handrick interrupted. "Do not sell them short, gentlemen, they are a force in and of themselves." 'Particularly when augmented by the larger breed and led by Weres who could communicate with them after a fashion,' he mentally added.

"I suppose we all need to know more before we can truly comment," offered Adermon, the engineer laying a cautionary hand upon the young officer's arm.

"Then what exactly are we facing? In the battle of Harrington Forge the Aldrigals fielded an army of sixty thousand," asked another young officer.

Lionel didn't recall his name either but thought he was from the von Tasir family.

"That was an army raised from the whole nation more than a century ago, and to be honest they could do that again if they had the time," answered Intona. "But the city itself is not so well guarded in peacetime. It takes time to raise and train an army and, frankly, the Aldrigal king has allowed his military to lapse."

"And why not?" offered Handrick. "With the fall of the Cafalstic Empire after the Were War they do not have any enemy states large enough or close enough to even consider attacking them."

"So what is their standing army?" Lionel asked, though he already knew the answer.

It was Intona who replied. He was obviously trying to regain some of his lost stature by appearing to be more knowledgeable than he truly was. He read from a report the duke himself had given him not an hour before.

"The nation of Aldrigal keeps no actual standing army, but the King himself has only a few hundred men guarding his palace. Each noble in the kingdom has their own troops the king can call upon but these are overwhelmingly mounted knights. In all there are at least twenty thousand heavy horsemen in the kingdom at this moment but it would take at least six weeks to gather enough of them for an organized battle. The city itself maintains a garrison of peacekeepers, most former soldiers but a sizeable portion of those are missing an arm or an eye lost in service to the king, of around five hundred, some of which are always away patrolling the roads. The residents of the Merchant's Quarter maintain an army of mercenaries that equal about the same amount. These are the most formidable defenders we would have to deal with."

"That's a lot of men," murmured the von Tasir officer.

"We can't hope to assault city walls that well defended," offered Barant.

"We won't have to," lectured Intona, rising to his full height. He may not be a master tactician but he could read quite well. "Our three-pronged attack will render the walls of Aldrigal useless."

More questions arose in an incomprehensible babble. It was Adermon who stood to his feet to calm the room.

"Perhaps you should just explain your plan, General."

Intona puffed up yet further, perhaps forgetting that the plan was not really his, and began.

"First we will have two companies of our regulars enter the city in small groups and take lodging in various inns throughout the city. Once in place they will wait until the proper time, following which they will gather in the city's two parks. From there, at midnight, one will take the Merchant's Quarter gates and the other the main city gates. Once our troops have possession of the gates the mercenary defenders will pull back to their employer's personal mansions and prepare to defend there, or simply run away."

This brought a nervous titter of laughter from the crowd. Jokes about the bravery of mercenaries were as common among regular soldiers as jokes about the stupidity of regular soldiers were among mercenaries.

"Why risk our regulars? Wouldn't mercenaries be better for that?" inquired a young Captain. Perhaps he was realizing why exactly he had been invited to such a high-level meeting. "No one would suspect a few mercenaries passing through, so long as they were in small groups. They could say that they're looking for work."

"Good question, Captain, but we do not consider the mercenaries as being all that reliable. When the time comes to pillage the city, they'll be there, but keeping their mouths shut while drinking during the waiting period is not something we wish to chance," Handrick announced.

Intona continued. "The gates need only hold against an assault of the peacekeepers, highly unlikely, or any unorganized rabble from among the peasantry that might rouse itself. Our people will then signal the second phase of our attack, which will consist of the bulk of our armed forces concealed in the nearby forest to enter the city. Once they get inside the city is ours."

"What of the third prong?" prompted Adermon.

"The third prong will consist of the Quargs and wolves. They will sweep around to the south clearing the road to Skallist and setting pickets to watch for any interference from that direction. Then they will march north and east to this point," he said, pointing to a spot on the map," and assault the King's Summer Palace."

"Why would he be there? It's hardly summer," stated Nira.

"He rarely leaves it these days; the king is getting up in years and finds that palace the most comfortable. At worst he might have traveled to Aldrigal City for something, but our informants will make sure that we know where he is; the odds say that he will be at the palace."

"Which will be the most heavily guarded place in Aldrigal," prompted Colonel Nira. "Defended with the best troops they have."

Handrick's laughter joined that of the duke's at the woman's response. "All you say is true," the Were stated, "but the finest offensive troops make poor defenders. Mounted Knights do poorly when defending walls. It will force them to dismount, at the least, and the walls of the palace are more ornamental than defensive. Also the Quargs will have the element of surprise, do no forget, and it is highly unlikely that more than a few dozen knights will even have time to arm themselves before our allies begin their slaughter."

"And the King will be ours at that point," stated the duke with a flourish, rising to his feet and taking instant command of the meeting. "With the city under our control and the king and most of the royal family dead or in chains it will be child's play to wrap up any resistance, leaving us in firm control of the kingdom, its trade routes, and its treasury. Within weeks of our attack, winter will descend upon the lowlands. This will be long before any legitimate armies can be raised to oppose us and any who do will have to deal with the cold and, eventually, snowfall."

All those hearing the plans for the first time looked stunned.

"This just might work. It just might," commented Colonel Mander, General Intona's aide.

"It will work, without question," replied the duke, not adding that if it didn't, their small nation was doomed. Being career military men, most of them anyway, they already knew what could happen to them personally if the attack failed.

Only Colonel Nira had any questions left to ask, speaking up to be heard over the excited babble. "When are we going to attack? And how are we going to get an army with sight of Aldrigal City without being seen? How will I be able to supply that many people on the far side of the Kenebruks?"

Her pessimism did nothing to lower the excitement of the officers. It was Lionel who replied.

"The attack will begin just after the harvest."

The babble died immediately.

"After the harvest? This year?" asked an incredulous Colonel Mander. "We're going to move an army of thousands over the Kenebruks with snow already falling on the high slopes, with supplies, and then prepare for an attack... in only a few weeks time?"

My Lord Adermon? This question is for you."

Standing to his feet Adermon cleared his throat before beginning.

"My Lord and Lady," he said, nodding in deference to Colonel Nira who snorted at his manners. She had beaten men for calling her a lady.

Ignoring her outburst the engineer continued. "Five years ago a patrol of Firthian border guards tracked a wounded bandit up into the mountains and there surprised the remainder of the band in a cave. Once the bandits were disposed of a few of the guards chanced further into the cave to explore. They found a relatively straight tunnel that traveled directly into the heart of the mountain, and a little further. Naturally they reported what they had found and orders were issued to seal the cave to prevent other bandits, or raiding Quargs, from using it in the future. All of this came to the attention of our beloved Duke, who had the far sight to see a greater potential for the cave."

Here Adermon paused; he knew exactly how Intona felt about being left out of all the planning for so long. "An engineer was dispatched to determine just how close the cave came to passing through the mountains," he said, an interested hum arising from the others as he spoke. "It was determined that the distance was not great; and so laborers were dispatched to begin cutting through. This has been accomplished."

This time Adermon allowed the murmuring to rise and spread for a few moments; letting the officers get it out of their system before he continued.

"A road was built between the foothills and the tunnel, and another began across the mountain. All the major obstacles have been overcome save one; a narrow but deep river that must be bridged. The pilings have been sunk and a serviceable crossing will be in place within the month. From there it is simply a matter of crossing the woodlands and entering the city."

Again everyone was jubilant, save Colonel Nira whose only concern was moving the necessary supplies.

"Wagons filled with food do not travel well in forest as thick as that. I have been to Aldrigal, Adermon, and those forests are not only thick but hilly as well." She turned her attentions to the duke. "Your Grace you have performed wonders in all that you've done, particularly in keeping it all a secret from Aldrigal, but this is a flaw that must be overcome."

The duke stood again, bowing slightly to Adermon and waiting until the engineer regained his seat before speaking.

"Colonel Nira, your concerns are well founded and have indeed been addressed. Laborers that survived the building and the tunnel, to be augmented by those who survive the building of the remaining bridge, are even now clearing timber. It is true that they will not be through the thickest of the forest in time to have your wagons with the army, but to do that would reveal our efforts too soon. Once they reach this point," he pointed to the map, "the army will forge ahead and storm the city."

"All this sounds wonderful, but the communications needed for such an attack will be difficult. How are we going to handle that?" asked Nira, no longer asking because she doubted the answer but out of curiosity as to how the issue had been resolved. She was now a believer, just like the other officers.

Lionel paced around the table to one of the side rooms and took the corner of the curtain in his hand.

"Another good question; it proves that you are all fine officers and a credit to your country. As before, however, this problem has also been anticipated and, hopefully, dealt with."

With that he pulled the curtain aside. Once the officers had a glimpse of what lay within, the final reservations ceased.

Chapter Fourteen

Gran sat in the chair much longer than she knew, devouring page after page until the book refused to allow her to turn any more. Backing up to the page marked by the ribbon, she began again in an effort to memorize all that she could. When she finished the second time, she was almost too stiff to stand, but did so amidst creaks and pops from all of her joints. Immediately upon standing, the chair and the book in her hands disappeared, the book reappearing on the shelf before her.

"Ach!" Gran said, jumping in surprise when the book vanished. Seeing it return to its place, she hesitantly touched it again and found herself able to remove it. As soon as she did, the chair returned. Curious she sat back down and then stood again, finding the book back on the shelf and the chair again missing.

Laughing she said, "That must be handy, like as not," to the room at large. She found it difficult to believe that all of this magic still worked without Istipol's consciousness being involved somehow. At least, that was the way that Gran thought that such magic must work.

Deciding that she would be able to return to the book whenever she was ready, Gran decided to pace a little before sitting back down. As she did so, she pulled a thick chunk of bread from the pocket of her shawl and ate, wanting to keep her strength up and mind sharp so as to learn as much as possible while she was here. For all that Gran knew, she might never be able to return.

The knowledge that Gran had so far discovered worried her. Much of it was only confusing gibberish as it referred to people and places that no longer existed or did so in a much different manner. One person in particular, a woman named Merceena, was mentioned many times in less than glowing terms. Istipol did not like Merceena, and suspected that this lack of respect was greatly returned. On nothing did the two women agree, and several examples were given. In her heart, Merceena was evil and at the time of writing that portion of the book Istipol was just beginning to both understand and accept this, despite some reputed earlier misgivings at the belief.

Not that the book was only about Istipol's thoughts. Much of it was devoted to notes and scribbles in the margins of different experiments and ideas that Istipol had. One paragraph was devoted to the just-received news concerning the death of Istipol's own mother, so this must have been many years before Gran's birth.

One entry truly intrigued Gran because it mentioned her own grandmother by name. She was described by Istipol as a 'mean-spirited grouch of a woman with a vile mouth and eternally venomous disposition'. The paragraph went on to say that Istipol respected the woman's hard work and qualities of loyalty. Istipol even admitted that 'she wished that she had a dozen servants like her,' although later she slightly recanted by saying 'I may have to promote her if I don't kill her first!' All in all, Gran was pleased with the description as they matched her own memories of the woman.

There was one page, written almost as a letter to someone, though no recipient was named. This gave Gran shivers down her spine when she first read it. She wasn't sure if the shivers had been magically induced or not, but each time she read the page it frightened her. If she cared to, Gran could believe that the letter had been written to her personally, but of course, that was foolishness. To think of someone being so specific in a letter written to someone that wasn't even have been born at the time...

In the letter, Istipol was cautioning 'the reader of this missive' to be careful in the pursuit of 'those who worship the moons'. Gran realized that anyone could be the 'reader' but then again, she had been pushed into reading this exact book. She was also cautious about just who exactly were 'those who worship the moons'. They might well be Weres as she had at first assumed, but there could be any number of cults dedicated to that particular worship. The world abounded with such foolishness.

Also in the letter Gran, who decided to read it as if it were meant solely for her, was warned against 'searching again for hearth and home' but instead to 'seek out the bud of iniquity and nip it there before it again takes root.' But what truly sealed the deal for Gran was a passage that read 'the cleanser that removes the stain will be that which cleansed it before' and later added 'those who cleanse are the Bearers of salvation in such evil times.' Although she didn't quite understand what it meant, something about the way it was written made it seem very true to her.

After carefully reading the book for a third time, Gran was surprised to find that it disappeared from her grasp even as she sat in the chair. When she tried to retrieve it from the shelf again, it would not budge. Upset at first, she decided to check nearby volumes to see if any others were now available. To her surprise she found a different one was available that had not been before; a book that was bound in yellow cloth with brown age spots, probably mold, now would allow itself to be removed. She again felt the delightful shiver down her spine when she touched it. Sitting back down in the chair, which was now yellow with brown spots to match the book, Gran found another ribbon marking a page, and began reading.

Almost the first thing she read was a memo from Istipol recording the names of her two newest apprentices. One was called 'Merceena', and notes accompanying this entry said that Istipol believed that the girl had given a false name. However, it seemed Istipol was not concerned about that and had chosen to accept the girl due to her 'raw but remarkable' skills with magic. Interesting, but not relevant to her problem, at least not in any way that Gran could determine. Obviously, this book was older than the first one.

The yellow book disappeared after but one reading, but the information had been limited. Only that single passage, of all that Gran had read, seemed to be pertinent to what she was looking for. The next book she was allowed to read was covered in red shaggy carpet and bound together by oversized metal hinges. It was ugly and ponderously heavy, but Gran was nothing if not stubborn. She struggled to get it into her lap and open it and eventually managed to do so.

The red book turned out to be the most interesting, but now Gran was getting sleepy. She stayed with it, however, and helped herself to a piece of dried beef from yet another pocket, hoping that the chewing, gumming would be more accurate, would help keep her focused. This book followed the same random order as the first two, with Istipol adding her thoughts and notations as they occurred and without any real identifiable order. Still, Gran found them all interesting, even fascinating, as they gave her an insight into the life of this famous person.

Six pages into the book, beginning where the ribbon allowed her to open it, Gran found something that made her sit up and caused all vestiges of sleep to flee from her eyes. In truth, she had not come here expecting something this specific. Her hopes had been to remove the library of Istipol from the list of possibilities. That Isitipol's personal symbol had shared common elements with the symbol from the Were medallion had been an accident, she was sure of it. Being allowed to enter the remains of the library had softened her disbelief somewhat, but still she had not expected to find anything extraordinary. Now she was looking at an exact copy of the Were medallion, drawn in the red book in Istipol's own hand.

Pulling the page from her pocket, Gran inspected it closely to be certain. It wasn't exact, but it was very close. Istipol had drawn the images at some point after Merceena had been asked to leave her service for unlisted indiscretions.

Istipol noted that Merceena had later taken a symbol to represent herself, as many Journeyman Magi did; it was something of a custom. Another common custom was to implement aspects of your master's symbol into your own, but Istipol had denied Merceena this right when she had asked her to leave. Somehow, Merceena had managed to complete her education in the magical arts and used the tree from Istipol's symbol anyway. Likely just to spite her former master, Istipol wrote.

Side by side, Istipol had drawn her own symbol and that of her former apprentice. Merceena had chosen to keep the tree, easily the largest and most recognizable portion of the symbol. This convinced Gran to agree with Istipol on Merceena's likely reasoning in using it. Spite was always easy to discern. The main differences between the two symbols lay along the edges of the trees. For Istipol's there were stars, moons, and other arcane images along with an open book and quills. At the base of Istipol's tree, the open book lay waiting for someone on a bed of grass. For Merceena's the base of the tree contained a tiny skull, something Gran had almost missed when first she copied the image, and the outside edge was covered with letters from an unknown language. According to Istipol's notes, the language was not familiar to her either but she believed it was a form of ancient Udrie, which was an offshoot of Elvish spoken by various evil humanoids a thousand years ago, long before the present age and any written records Gran had ever heard of.

Gran sniffed. That last didn't help much, unless she met a thousand year old evil humanoid inclined to translate for her. Istipol did identify two of the runes as Elvish but that told Gran little that she didn't already know.

Istipol went on to say that she believed Merceena had completed her education somewhere and had built some type of research facility in the wilderness to the west of Skallest. Istipol did not know the purpose of the facility but she did surmise that it had been chosen because of its remote location.

"Nothing good ever came from Skallest, like as not," Gran told herself.

After Gran read that portion twice and copied Istipol's notes onto her own drawing of the symbol, the red book vanished, along with the chair. Gran sat down hard on the floor, which suddenly turned icy cold. The light in the room dimmed drastically as Gran sat shivering on the floor. Apparently, she was finished with her research. Gathering her things that had scattered as she fell, Gran returned the way that she had come.

Chapter Fifteen

Gran awoke fresh and clear-headed after being little more than a dead-head the previous day. She had spent a great deal longer in the remnants of the library than she had believed and had paid for it in the two nights since.

Leaving the library had been no problem; it was obvious to her that she was no longer welcome there. Her first steps into the tunnels had caused her to step on the sleeping Cora's hair. She had followed that up by stepping to one side at Cora's cry only to kick Kelendle in the nose with the back of one heel. After berating the pair for sleeping on the cold stone floor in the darkness, Gran ordered them to lead her back to the Jackdog as quickly as they could. By the time they returned, Kelendle was worried that he might have to carry Gran up the secret stairs, so exhausted was the old woman. Somehow, she had made it by leaning on Cora; the frail girl had proven remarkably strong and resilient, but it had been tough going.

Now that she had finally caught up on her sleep, she felt ready to see to certain arrangements. Her morning was lost as she did not awake until well past noon and was content to spend most of the afternoon mending her traveling clothes and pondering all that she had learned in the library. By the time the evening began she was famished and went to the dinning room looking forward to another dish of souse. There she was served by Cora and dinner was spent in conversation with Kelendle. The man seemed willing to help Gran in any way that he could. It was obvious that he took his vow to help anyone who knew the secret family sign very seriously.

"Did you find the information you sought, Gran?" Kelendle had asked.

Gran was always careful what she shared but Kelendle deserved to have some of his curiosity appeased.

"Yes, I found more than I expected, thanks to you and young Cora."

"And Gran, if I could, what exactly did you find?"

Gran knew that he didn't mean the information she found. He wanted to know what lay beyond the door that he, his father, nor even his grandfather had guarded but never been allowed to pass through.

She had taken her time, and explained what the inner rooms had looked like and even described some of the books she had seen there. She told of the chair that appeared when a book was taken from a shelf, but didn't divulge her misadventures concerning the shocks or the disappearing chair that had dropped her on her backside. Some things didn't need to be shared. Such an omission in another would have earned them a stern lecture on the sin of pride but Gran realized that in her case, it was simply not pertinent information and so had left it out.

"Truly amazing," the man had said in wonder.

Gran's return questions about the hidden doors they had passed on the way to the library had been rebuffed.

"I'm sorry Gran, but my vow will not allow me to share that," Kelendle had apologized.

She hadn't expected anything else, but pretended to be hurt anyway.

"So what do you do now, Gran?" Kelendle had asked, not only to change the subject but also to find out if she needed anything else from him. It was exciting to meet such a fascinating and mysterious woman, particularly when she was a relative and the first to know the secret sign of their family in years, but in some ways Kelendle knew that he would be glad when she left. He smelled trouble on the woman and the Jackdog didn't need any new sources of that.

"I need to leave as soon as I can get supplies. Not tomorrow, but the next day, like as not."

Kelendle nodded. "If you will give me a list of the supplies you need, I'll make sure that Cora puts them together for you tomorrow."

"I thank you, Kelendle. You have been very supportive of this old woman."

"Just honoring my vow, Gran."

Gran sniffed. "Honoring a vow to a dead man is well enough, I suppose, but you should be sure the people you help are worth the effort."

Smiling Kelendle replied, "I try, Gran."

The two had fallen silent as Gran's souse arrived and was placed before her. She hadn't realized how much she had missed the recipe.

Once they were alone, Kelendle asked, "If I may know, where will you be traveling to?" Seeing the look on Gran's face, he held up a hand in placation. "I only ask so that I can be as helpful to you as possible."

"It might be better if you didn't know, boy," Gran had sniffed, donning her most imperious air, "there are things you don't know that could be a problem for you later."

Reaching into a pocket of the sequined vest he wore, Kelendle pulled out a folded sheet of parchment. Handing it to Gran he said, "I doubt that anything you haven't told me would change my feelings over my offer."

Gran reluctantly put down her fork and took the parchment, unfolding it and laying it upon the table. It was a wanted poster with a badly drawn caricature of her face featured prominently upon it.

"Ah, so you know about this, do you? I apologize for the risk to your family." She stared at it a moment. "Why did they draw me with my mouth open?"

Kelendle had waved the apology away. "You are family, Gran, no matter how distant you may be in blood. Besides," he laughed, "You're not the first wanted criminal we've concealed on the premises."

"Then you'll oblige me by not asking who it was that I'm supposed to have murdered?" Gran demanded, fixing her gaze on the man.

Kelendle held up his hands defensively. "Of course, Gran. I'm sure they deserved it." Gran noticed that he didn't bother to protest that she could not have committed murder.

Gran nodded once. "They did that, boy. I'm sorry I can't tell you more but there are others involved that I can't risk."

She ate in silence as Kelendle sipped sparingly from a mug of ale. Once her bites slowed, though she had yet to finish even a quarter of the loaf, he leaned towards her to continue in a low voice.

"Gran, I'm a man who can keep his mouth shut. My life and the lives of my family depend on it, as does the livelihood of my family. If you would trust me with your destination, I believe that I can help you along the way."

Pushing away her platter Gran leveled a long stare at Kelendle. They both knew that revealing her destination was risky. Knowing where she was going would make it child's play for the authorities to find her if someone wanted to turn her in for the reward money. An ancient crone riding on a donkey would not be a difficult person to chase down by a squad of the King's Horsemen.

For that matter, if Kelendle wanted to turn her in for the reward, he could arrange it so that she was picked up along the street when she left the Jackdog. No one would suspect Kelendle of doing it if it happened away from his establishment, at least no open accusations would be leveled, and so his reputation among the local thieves would not be damaged. Gran normally relied on her instincts and gut feelings; they were as much a part of her as her intelligence. She felt good about Kelendle, more so than she ever had about his great-grandfather, whom she had despised, and so simply did what felt right.

"I will be going to Skallest, like as not. At least in that direction. I'm not sure what my destination is exactly but that is the first step."

Kelendle immediately brightened, the serious look on his face fading to a brilliant smile. "That's good news, Gran, because I think I know someone who can help you."

The man was excited, but obviously asking for Gran's permission before continuing with his offer. Gran knew that innkeepers learned early to allow others to do the talking and only interject when asked or if absolutely necessary.

"Go on, I'm listening," Gran replied, not liking the thought of someone else being brought into a confidence she had barely decided to allow Kelendle into.

"Actually two people. A married couple; friends of mine and trustworthy besides. You have my word on that," Kelendle explained, talking quickly as if expecting to be interrupted.

Sipping her milk, Gran peered over the rim of her cup. "And why would I need these people?"

"They are going to Skallest as well, Gran. They would be able to help you along the way."

Sitting her cup down with a solid thump that slopped milk out onto the table, Gran glared at the man. "Why do I need someone to help me ride along a road?" she scoffed. "Does the road periodically wander away from its destination? Perhaps someone might want to rob me for my riches? Or perhaps they want to steal me away for my beauty?"

Kelendle looked at the tabletop in embarrassment. "Gran, I was just thinking that you might be a little... easy to spot," he offered. "You are wanted, and there is a price on your head. You are not someone who is easily overlooked. However, if you were to travel with someone else, say in a wagon masquerading as a servant, you might just get out of the city without being caught."

Her glare was in place simply out of habit. Within her mind, Gran was mulling the man's words and finding them making a great deal of sense. If Gran had a fault, and she would never admit to anyone much less herself that she did, it might be that she was not inclined to avoid people's attention.

In the end, she had at least agreed to meet the couple that Kelendle spoke of. Gran was naturally ready to meet with them right then but Kelendle urged her to wait until tomorrow.

"I can arrange for you all to share the noon meal together. You can come in alone and leave alone. In this booth," the red-haired man looking meaningfully about them, "no one will be able to see you together or overhear your conversation. You can get to know them and decide for yourself whether or not to travel with them."

Gran nodded, satisfied with the precautions. Meeting with the couple in a room might look suspicious to an employee or patron of the Jackdog who chanced upon Gran entering or leaving a room not her own. People were unlikely to notice guests of the inn going to the dining room at mealtime. Only their server would know who or how many people were in one of the private alcoves and Gran felt comfortable about trusting Cora. Typically Gran did have one useful suggestion to the plan.

"I will meet with them, Kelendle, because you have vouched for them, but why must we wait until noon tomorrow? Why not now? Or over breakfast first thing in the morning?"

Kelendle looked abashed. "I'm sorry Gran but I doubt that that would be possible. This couple doesn't usually come down for breakfast, and rarely make it for the noon meal either."

His words surprised Gran, though she was more surprised at her own surprise than confused as to why a married couple might wish to remain in their rooms past noon. Too many years getting up with the chickens had tricked Gran into forgetting that not everyone was an early riser. She thought perhaps that Kelendle wasn't being entirely truthful with her, but was instead using a tactic Gran herself often employed; allowing people to believe what they wanted to without actually admitting to anything. Gran reluctantly accepted it. As many secrets as Gran kept from others, she certainly couldn't begrudge Kelendle one of his own. Either she trusted him or she didn't, and this was a time for trust. 'Trust whom ye must and keep your noggin-knocker handy,' was an old saying Gran was fond of repeating. Gran thanked Kelendle again for his help and suggestions, agreeing to meet with the couple at noon.

"But see to it that the lay-a-bouts aren't late; I can't be wasting the whole day waiting for them to wake up," she groused, just to remain in character. She was, after all, an old peasant woman who had lived her whole life on a farm or in a backwoods village.

"I'll see to it, Gran. They won't be late."

Chapter Sixteen

Gran awoke, dressed early and made her way downstairs well before the sun was up. She stopped by the rooms where the kitchen help slept to roust out the morning staff to start fixing her breakfast. They had become accustomed to this crazy old woman's demands and gladly obeyed to keep the sharp edge of her tongue from lashing them. Once they were busy to her satisfaction, she sat at what had become her usual table and placed her breakfast order with the sleepy servant that followed her there. In record time for the kitchen of the Jackdog, two eggs were fried to perfection and joined on a platter with a bowl of steaming mush and placed on the table before her.

"I will have my breakfast delivered to my room or you shall feel the wrath of the House of Gelbow!" came an imperiously demanding voice, startling Gran from the contemplation of her morning eggs. Normally she would inspect them closely for any perceived imperfections but the voice had diverted her attention.

Leaning over Gran nudged the curtains aside so that she could peer between them, finding the impending argument simply too tempting not to watch. There were only two people in sight, two women, standing in front of the door to the kitchens.

"Mistress, we do not serve meals in the rooms, you'll have to come down here," explained the plump middle-aged woman who was in charge of the kitchens. Cora had explained that the woman was her mother's sister.

"You'll serve me where I command you to," snarled the tiny woman who opposed the kitchen overseer, hands on her fists and her nose as high as she could lift it. From behind she looked to be no older than Cora, but the imperiousness in her voice was that of someone much older. Someone used to being obeyed.

"But Mistress, I have just explained to you..." began the overseer, only to again be interrupted.

"Fetch the owner, immediately," the little woman demanded, forcing the servant to give way before her. The overseer finally bowed and fled the room, leaving the way clear for Gran to inspect this woman whose mouth was larger than her body.

Tiny she was, perhaps shorter than Gran, whose age had long ago bowed her back. She was beautiful in a cold sort of way, with oversized eyes and more hair than should be able to find purchase on so small a head. A brilliant blonde in color, the hair extended out from the woman almost like a halo or a mane, and hung well down her thin back. Although she could not see from her vantage point, Gran was sure that the woman had pointed ears as well.

"An Elf, like as not," Gran stated to no one in particular. The servant who had brought her eggs had used the disturbance to flee the dining room and so avoid being scolded by Gran for some imagined insult in the breakfast she had brought.

Gran noticed that the Elf was well dressed, wearing clothing of more value than all the shawls and linen shifts Gran had ever owned. Her blouse was made of pale green silk, if Gran didn't miss her guess, with overlarge puffy sleeves that ended just below the elbow. A colorful sash of darker green wound around the woman's midriff, above silken breeches of an even darker shade of green and on her feet were slippers, also made of silk but lined with fur and unaccountably blue in color. These were not the clothes of someone just getting up but rather those of someone just getting home from a late night.

The Elf stalked back and forth across the floor of the large dining hall, muttering to herself and glaring at the single person who dared to enter the room while she did so. The young boy forgot whatever his task had been and darted back into the kitchens with a cry. Somehow, this pleased the Elf, who smiled thinly at the performance.

Gran had forgotten all about her food as she watched the Elf pace angrily. Quite quickly in Gran's estimation, Kelendle arrived in the kitchen, only half dressed and eyes red from sleep. He immediately bowed to the Elf and apologized for whatever offense his staff had caused. She could tell that the poor man wasn't the least clear on what trouble he had been called upon to repair.

"I demand that our morning meal be delivered to our room immediately," the Elf demanded, snapping one arm as if she held a whip. Kelendle flinched as if she did.

"Of course, My Lady, it will be brought up straightaway!"

Gratified for the moment the Elf stalked from the room as if on her way to right another universal injustice. She left a dazed Kelendle to deal with his wife's aunt, who was already arguing with his decision.

"You said no meals in the rooms, Kelendle. You said it yourself, and I was doing just what you said!" she shrilled, pointing a chubby finger in his face. The woman likely had no idea that she had adopted the elven woman's stance and mannerisms as she dressed her brother-in-law down.

Dropping the curtain back across her alcove Gran left Kelendle to mollify his employees and customers while she ate her breakfast. She had wolfed down most of her food before she even remembered to check it for any inadequacies. So much had she enjoyed the little tirade that Gran forgot to even be angry when she left the dining room, and wished a startled servant a pleasant 'good day' as she climbed the stairs.

By midmorning Gran had nearly forgotten the morning's entertainment. The whole event had seemed little more than a humorous diversion. It was back on her mind when she returned to the alcove for her noon meal to find Kelendle there before her and asked if she wouldn't mind meeting his friends in their room as they had chosen to have all their meals served there this day. Suddenly looking suspicious, Gran agreed but only after repeating all her previous misgivings about being seen entering the couple's room.

"It'll be of little use to sneak out when everyone in the place knows I was in their rooms just before they left," she grouched. "I'll not even get out of the city before they take me, like as not."

Kelendle's face showed no emotion at the woman's words even as he thought to himself how much he pitied anyone trying to arrest Gran.

"So this couple I'm meeting; the woman is an elf, isn't she?" Gran demanded, keeping her voice down as she fixed her better eye on the tall man. Kelendle kept his vision fixed on the tabletop as he answered.

"She is, Gran. I guess you were already up when she came in here this morning."

"Up I was, and the best part of the day it is," she stated, glaring at the innkeeper as if waiting for him to argue with her. "And what sort of lay-a-bouts have you gotten me mixed up with? That woman was just getting home!"

"She was, or rather they were, Gran. She and her husband are quite infamous for their... uh... leisure activities."

Gran snorted to reveal her thoughts about that subject. Parties were fine when there was no work to do but Gran had yet to find a single moment when there wasn't some work available for idle hands.

"Wastrels, slothful and incapable of an honest day's work," Gran sniffed. "Which means they don't have an honest coin to their names, like as not, and elves besides! People like them can't be trusted, Kelendle, you mark my words. When the going gets tough they'll tell all that they know; about me, about you, and anything else they can think of. Don't put any faith in them, boy, take my word for it."

Kelendle smiled at her outrage, and being referred to as 'boy', and replied, "Gran only the woman is an elf, her husband is as human as I am, and you have my word that they can be trusted; they've both been good friends of mine for a long time."

Not wanting to snort again so soon, that habit had earned her the nickname 'porker' as a child, something it had taken her decades to outlive, Gran simply rolled her eyes at Kelendle's naiveté. "Friends that only occasionally show up on your doorstep to drink and gamble are not to be trusted! Particularly not when one is an elf and both are of the nobility. I've lived long enough to know that elves are too flighty to be reliable and have heads full of nonsense while the noble-born are too lazy to turn their hands to an honest day's work and don't have a creative thought in their simple little minds," she scoffed, grabbing up her mug of water and sipping from it just so she could glare at the innkeeper over the rim.

"Well, you may have him down pretty well but you've missed your guess on her," Kelendle said, continuing to smile broadly. "She's not the least bit flighty and has a head filled with common sense; you two will get along well I'm certain. Lord Jamus and Lady Eldena are the Viscount and Viscountess of Gelbow. His title is hereditary and he is quite the spoiled rich brat but she is something else entirely, Gran. Eldena is not what she appears and has some magical training. For that matter, Jamus is steadier than he appears; I'd trust either of them with my life and, as a matter of fact, have."

Gran nodded once to show her acceptance of Kelendle's words; she might not be as gullible as the innkeeper but she recognized that the man had a good head on his shoulders. He needed to convince her and so he had; now it was time to meet these spoiled, rich brats.

"I'll meet them, like I said that I would. I'm not surprised that our good, common sense plans had to be changed because your friends had to sleep in. Nobles and elves being reliable and trustworthy... hah!"

Kelendle accepted the rebuke and led Gran from the dining room and up the main stairs. Gran noticed two of Kelendle's 'servers' loitering on the stairs as they climbed; neither man even met their boss' eyes but Gran knew that they were there for a reason; either to keep people from seeing her enter the noble's room or ensuring that the right people did. You could never be too sure.

The wooden stairs were carpeted so their climb was noiseless if you discounted Gran's grunts and gasps as she struggled up the incline. The hum of conversation and other sounds from the kitchens died quickly away and the relative silence Gran loved about the Jackdog settled around them. Gripping Kelendle's offered arm like a tree root digging through a rock, Gran made the climb only having to stop twice to catch her breath. Kelendle stayed with her all the way to the third floor, the top save for the attic where Kelendle's family lived, ignoring the pain from the old woman's grip.

The third storey having been reached, Kelendle led Gran past her own room to the last of the three doors on the level. Behind them one of the guards appeared to lean against the railing of the stairs as he casually watched for anyone who might appear. Kelendle knocked once and, his duties as guide complete, left to return to the front desk. He recognized the look on Gran's face and didn't want to suffer if her meeting with the nobles did not go well.

Gran waited a few seconds before pushing her way into the room. She had failed to hear the mumbled invitation from inside but didn't feel the least bit unsure of bursting in whether anyone had invited her or not. She wanted to be inside the room before Kelendle reached the stairs.

The room was richly appointed, more than the equal of the one that Gran had been given. Between those two rooms and one other, they occupied the entire third floor of the Jackdog. The bed was a massive affair; four thick posts supported a canopy that looked like a famous scene from another Jackdog fable. It depicted a hunting scene of hounds in pursuit of a stag who was in turn pleading with the Jackdog for help. That story had turned out badly for the hunters as well as the stag, which had in the end rejected the terms demanded by the Jackdog after the hunters had been dealt with. Not the best possible omen for their meeting. The rest of the room was filled with carpets and tapestries and even the chamber pot was made of ivory. Kelendle had few rooms this richly appointed, but anyone who could afford them was well cared for indeed.

Reclining on the bed lay a man with a wet cloth draped across his forehead, his eyes tightly shut and his sweaty coal-black hair splayed about the pillow. The skin visible on his face and hands was as soft as the silken sheets he lay upon, and it was obvious to Gran that he had never spent a day working in the sun. He was as human as was Gran, which of course didn't surprise her, but the sheer softness of his appearance certainly did.

Sitting on one edge of the bed was the Elf, so far refusing to acknowledge Gran's presence in the room. She was carefully rubbing a short, flat stick across each of her fingernails in turn, smoothing the edges. Her mother had had one of those little sticks. They were covered in fine sand or some other type of grit. With each slide of nail across stick the man in the bed would wince as if someone where drilling a hole in his head. That was all Gran needed to diagnose his illness. The man was suffering from the age-old disease that always followed a night of heavy drinking.

That they were man and wife was surprising. A couple, certainly possible, but a full marriage between the two races was uncommon. Even if Kelendle's assertion that the elf had not been born to the nobility was correct, and the way the woman held herself denied it, the man most obviously was and providing an heir had always been important to such as they. All knew that Elves and humans could not produce offspring. There was a story here to be heard. A woman from Kelendle's staff was busy soaking a cloth in cool water to replace the one on the man's brow. Gran barely had time for a quick scan of the room before the elf spoke.

"Master Kelendle says that you will be traveling with us," the Elf said, breaking the silence. The man on the bed groaned pitifully at her words.

"Silence, I beg of you," he whined.

Gran measured her response, clearly not liking the presence of the servant. "I was told the same thing. Not sure if I'm going to accept yet."

"Our names are Lord Jamus and Lady Eldena. We are the Viscount and Viscountess of Gelbow. We are genteel born and expect to be maintained in the manner to which we are accustomed."

Gran didn't bother to measure anything this time. "You can expect anything you want to. Doesn't mean it'll happen," she sniffed.

The Elf looked up, studying the old human crone. It was the first time she had truly looked at Gran since the woman entered the room. "You will be my maid and care for my effects." Gran may not have even spoken for all the reaction she gave. "I am a harsh task-mistress who will accept nothing less than perfection in my servants. When we reach Skallest you will be paid and allowed to go on your way. Until then you will obey me or suffer my wrath."

Swelling up to her full height Gran stared down her nose at the little Elf. She had never taken this type of abuse from Lord Ferule and she'd be branded as a goblin if she was going to take it from an Elf with hair taller than herself.

"Look here, missy, I know what you are and what you expect, but let me set you straight on a few details! My name is Gran, and if I agree to travel with you it will not be as your servant! Not that I'm above caring for those who can't care for themselves, but you look plenty fit to me!"

The man groaned at the steadily rising pitch of Gran's voice. "Mercy, dear lady," he begged.

"You shut up and lay there, boy; you deserve every pain you're suffering, like as not." She turned back on the Elf. "If I travel with you it will be because I choose to, and for no other reason. Kelendle arranged this because he thought he was helping me. I'm traveling to Skallest whether or not you young shags come!"

Gran continued on in fine voice, so intent on her words that she failed to notice the Elf's reaction. The diminutive woman jumped from the bed and stalked over to Gran. The only reaction from the older woman was to add a wagging finger to her words, either to emphasize her words or to keep some distance between them even Gran wasn't sure. She had no chance to avoid the stinging slap the Elf delivered to her cheek.

Shocked into silence for perhaps the first time in her life, Gran stopped in mid-word looking remarkably like the picture of herself on the wanted poster. Her face turned red, then even redder as she gathered her strength. The servant dropped her pan of cool water and fled the room, shrieking for Kelendle. Balling up one fist Gran reached for her ever-ready switch in one pocket and studied her opponent. There was no give in the Elf's eyes, but then again, there had never been any in Gran's.

Chapter Seventeen

Among the legends of Aldrigal are several concerning incredible battles. Wars and clashes of armies and even stunning victories of smaller forces over larger ones abound in the rich history of both the city and the nation. For six years, the city was besieged by the armies of Maltroc the Maddog and twice invasions were defeated in street-to-street fighting by the citizens of the city. Even the Jackdog in his fables was said to have been a participant in combat at times. All of those were said to be inconsequential, though, when compared to the spat between the two visitors of the Jackdog Inn when they met on the uppermost public floor one afternoon.

Shrieks and screams were punctuated by the crash of glass and the sound of breaking furniture. Curses in Elvish were largely incomprehensible to those who witnessed the battle but those shouted in the local tongue were so strong as to cause teamsters to flush with embarrassment.

Not that anyone actually witnessed the fight first hand other than a stunned Lord Gelbow who was seen fleeing down the stairs with a nasty cut on one temple and a stunned look of stark fear on his face. Kelendle was the only person who dared to go up, and he quickly returned, his face ashen and his eyes haunted from what he had seen.

"They're killing each other," he had whispered, and then posted a guard at the foot of the stairs to augment those already further up. "No one goes up until someone is dead," he said, before going to the bar to join Lord Gelbow in a stiff drink.

"Will the old one back down?" the Viscount had asked Kelendle.

"No sooner than will your wife," was Kelendle's response, his words punctuated by the crash of a flying plate.

The crashes stopped before the curses did, Kelendle figured that they must have run out of dishes and furniture to throw at one another, but the verbal sparring went on for some time, along with the occasional meaty 'thwacks' of an open-handed slap. When silence suddenly descended upon the inn, it was almost more frightening than the fight had been.

"They've killed each other," one teamster declared, doubling his bet with an enterprising cooper who was laying even odds on the combatants for one or the other to lose outright or, the most popular bet of the day, that both would be knocked unconscious or dead. These betting lines were surprisingly easy to sell when none of the bettors really had any but the vaguest of ideas who they were betting on. Only the kitchen staff and the servant who had been present at the start of the trouble had any insight to give, and Kelendle worked hard to keep her from talking. However, the sounds of the battle were simply too interesting to pass up and a number of regulars wagered as much as a day's pay on the outcome. With baited breath, the crowd in the common room sat staring at the stairs, waiting to see who would come down. Eventually, the wait became too much and the crowd demanded that Kelendle check on the outcome. Taking Lord Gelbow by the arm for support, the two men climbed the two flights of stairs to check for survivors.

Reaching the top floor, which fortunately only had two occupied rooms; Gran's and that of the Lord and Lady Gelbow, Kelendle was upset to see every visible piece of furniture and vase broken or smashed. Even the picture frames and tapestries had been pulled down there in the hall. Thankfully, the doors had all been locked, so likely the devastation didn't extend beyond Lord Gelbow's room. The guard who had been on the third floor at the beginning of the fight now stood with his companion on the safer second, and was looking up the stairs open-mouthed when Kelendle passed him.

"I ain't never seen nothing like that," he murmured. "Those women are crazy."

The Viscount still looked ashen from his drinking bout the night before, and the morning's events hadn't done him any good. He pushed Kelendle on ahead of him as he fingered the silken sash of the sleeping robe he still wore. The two approached the open door of the Viscount's room cautiously, prepared to duck a flung vase or chamber pot if necessary. There they found the pair of combatants sitting on the floor of the room amid a swath of destruction, glaring at one another from arm's length at most. Neither was blinking as they stared, and the faces of both were purple with bruises.

Watching from the safety of the doorway, the two men shared whispered ideas about what had happened. Kelendle thought they were bewitched while the Viscount believed that they were locked in a 'stubborn contest' of such proportions that time itself had stopped in the room. After a long period of time, it was the Viscountess who broke the silence.

"So we're agreed then?"

"Aye, we're agreed," Gran responded. Neither were even out of breath, although Gran did look tired.

"This is the best way to handle the situation."

"No doubt about it."

Reaching out a hand the two women shook on their agreement, sharing a small smile. As one they looked towards the doorway and the two men.

"Everything is set, we leave in the morning," the Viscountess stated.

"The people downstairs think we're crazy too, like as not," added Gran.

"They do that," stammered the Viscount. "Whatever were you two doing?"

"Simply establishing our alibi. No one will expect us to be leaving together, particularly since we obviously hate one another," the Lady explained. "The local thieves that have been watching the Jackdog in recent days will not suspect Gran to be among our entourage."

"I will of course be recuperating in my room for several days, being a feeble old woman and all," Gran cackled. "Unfortunately, my sweet little donkey will have to be left behind and such a pity that will be."

"And I will be upset at the insult allowed to be visited upon my person by a common street hag within this hovel of an inn and so will be intent upon leaving at first light."

"I suppose that I will be similarly upset but will pay for the damages simply to sweep this whole sordid scene under the rug?" sighed the Viscount, rolling his eyes and then hanging his head in resignation.

The two women smiled.

Kelendle raised a hand. "This was all staged? And who is watching the Jackdog? I'm on good terms with the local cartels and pay good money for them to stay away. Who and why are they watching?"

Standing up from her sitting position in one fluid motion the elf stretched to work the kinks from her back. "I saw various street thugs watching the Jackdog so I used my abilities to find out what they wanted, just in case it was to waylay my dear husband and I," she said, walking over and stroking the vapid face of the Viscount. "Apparently Gran was noticed on her way here and when the wanted posters were issued someone remembered. A reward that could easily be picked up when she left."

Kelendle growled. "I'll take care of the watchers."

Gran struggled to her feet using her walking staff to lever herself upright. "Are you daft, boy? We've taken care of it already! By the time they realized that I'm not taken abed in my room we'll be long gone. It's to my advantage that they watch."

"I don't understand any of this," moaned the Viscount, slumping down to sit on the bed. Apparently it had been the only piece of furniture too large to break.

Hobbling over to Kelendle Gran poked a finger into his chest. "I'm going to my room to moan and groan a while, you tell everyone downstairs that this persnipity little elf has horribly injured this sweet little old woman who wanted nothing more than to hire on as a servant."

"Hah!" sang out the elf. "Better yet tell them that I have put the lowly peasant woman in her place once and for all!"

Gran joined in her laughter. "Oh, and you'd better send for a healer," she added, then seeing the look on Kelendle's face added, "Don't worry, I can fake enough injuries to fool some backstreet charlatan."

"You arranged all of this in advance? When?"

"This morning, after breakfast," cackled Gran. "This little elf is surprisingly resourceful when it comes to communication."

"I have a small measure of magical talent in that regard," replied the Viscountess.

"My dear you promised," whined the Viscount, draping a blanket around his shoulders. "You said we could enjoy a bit of travel for once without all of this adventuring nonsense."

The elf stepped to her husband's side and held his head to her breast. "You were the one who told Kelendle we would help Gran out of the city, were you not? I simply arranged for your promise to be possible."

Hobbling out of the room Gran motioned for Kelendle to leave. "You'll need to tell the bettors who won," she smiled, moving towards the door to her own bedroom.

Kelendle stepped through the door after her, to do as he had been told but stopped and swiveled his head back and forth between the two women.

"Was all this really necessary?" he asked.

Looking at one another through the open doorway the two women laughed again.

"Perhaps not, but it certainly was fun!" said the elf.

Chapter Eighteen

As trails go this one had been tricky. It had taken weeks to arrive in Aldrigal and more time had been lost searching the area of the Were attack with little or no success. No Weres had been found and no sign had been seen of the old woman Lord Burstis had been sent to find. At least there had not been before today. If things went well, the quarry might be taken this very night.

With the wanted posters already being circulated prior to the agent's arrival it was a wonder the old hag had not already been captured. In truth the agent had expected to find this 'Gran' safely rotting in someone's dungeon by now. It was a pity but this task would need to be accomplished the hard way. A suitable application of gold had eased the search but it had still been more difficult that it should have been.

Autumn was soon to be hard upon the land and in the far north where the agent had been born snow would surely be falling soon. If his brother still lived he would hunting the black mok already, harvesting the thick fur for sale in the spring. Deer would already be getting thinner, and would not be the first choice for prey now. Here a few of the trees were only beginning to turn while most still stood green and proud. Snow was preferable for hunting. The prey was often easy to take when hibernating or slowed by the snow drifts, and usually had fattened up in preparation of the long sleep. Not that one old woman would be any challenge.

Stopping the horse the agent dismounted and knelt to the ground, sniffing at the spoor there for a hint of what might lay ahead. The beast stamped a hoof nervously but did not shy away. It was too well trained for that. Trained to tolerate the presence of a Were as well as being bred to speed and stamina. The Duke of Firth equipped his agents well, in horseflesh and other equipment.

Horses by the scent, humans of both sexes, he decided. Perhaps an elf, though their scent was more difficult to detect. The tracks revealed a wheeled conveyance of some type, pulled by six massive draft horses. The various bits of information seemed to confirm that these were his prey, if the hoof prints found here belonged with the carriage tracks he had found. At this point the wheel tracks could have belonged to a farmer's cart, though they looked too wide for something so simple, and the horses could have been herded along by a fellow seeking to sell them in the city; the ground was too hard and the horses too heavy to tell if they were being ridden. Lord Burstis recognized all the possibilities but doubted them all. This was his prey, he felt sure.

Of all places the prey, Gran, had turned up in the capitol city of Aldrigal itself. It had seemed more likely that a simple peasant woman would flee to another small village or along the nearest road but this one had not, choosing instead to try and disappear within the largest city in this part of the world. It was surprising and had almost worked for that very reason. Agents of the Duke of Firth had found her purely by accident. A child of the streets, one of the thieving little urchins every sizeable city was infested with, had recognized the old hag as she entered a section of the city near the Merchant's Quarter. Coins paid to a street gang had eventually revealed her hiding place in an old inn and more of the same had kept the establishment under watch. Almost the old woman had escaped the city unseen.

But Lord Burstis was better than that. Common street ruffians might accept the rumors of the woman's being injured and trying to recover at the inn, but he took no such chances. If the old woman was still at the Jackdog, all well and good, but Burstis had hired some local thugs to follow the nobles anyway; just in case something else was going on. Similar agents hired to verify Gran's presence inside the Jackdog had been difficult to hire and the one willing man Burstis found was discovered floating face down in the river the next morning. Fortunately Burstis had not had to risk himself in an assault on the inn; keeping the Curse hidden in such a situation would have been difficult and Lord Firth had been very clear that no sign of any Were could be allowed to arise.

Following the popinjay and his lace and powder wife had been easily accomplished, particularly when they were away from the influence of the Jackdog's owner. A single day's travel outside the city the agents of Lord Burstis had caught sight of Gran hiding within the wagon and reported back. Now it was only a matter of time before he caught up to the slow moving wagon. Only a matter of a few hours now, if the spoor here was not corrupted in some way.

It was a simple plan. Catch up to the wagon, verify the prey, and then stop the wagon on some pretext. If the wagon was too well guarded, wait until night and take the old woman then. If the wagon was poorly defended, the agent would not have to wait but could attack and then kill at leisure, so long as he ensured that there were no survivors and he left no evidence that a Were had been involved in the conflict. Easily accomplished tasks in such a remote area. Three days travel out of the city even lone farms became rare and Lord Burstis had yet to see a second hovel on this day.

A few more hours and Gran would be helpless and begging for the chance to tell the Burstis whatever was asked. Even the location of her so-called 'dead' grandson.

Chapter Nineteen

A cooling breeze dropped off the mountains that, at least for today, felt good to the sweating laborers working to fill the hole. This latrine had filled up in record time and another had already been dug. Before them lay the hastily prepared road, easily marked by the rows of tree stumps that marched away through the forest. Behind them the hilltop was dotted with small two-man tents and, further back, the larger tents that marked the commanders. Beyond these larger tents were rows of wagons ready to transport the supplies when needed. Horses and mules milled about in a brush-fence corral, unconcerned with the plight of the starving workers as they happily fed on the hay being forked over the fence to them. Here on the eastern side of the Kenebruks the weather was better than what they army had left beyond the mountains, but it was obvious that winter was well on its way.

Handrick cared nothing for the plight of the laborers; they were nearly all dead now and had no use beyond felling a few more trees. The bridge, a week past due, had finally been completed and the road advanced nearly as far as they dared before the attack. Quargs in small parties were sweeping up a few woodsmen who, despite the wolf attacks of last year, had begun creeping back into the area. These Aldrigalians were like rats, Handrick had decided. You just couldn't kill enough of them.

He passed well around the laborers because he couldn't abide their smell. It wasn't the sweat or even the filth they were caked in, no one in the camp had bathed in months; it was the fear and hopelessness that made him ill. Those men had all given up their hopes and were just waiting to die; no prey he hunted would smell that way.

"Have the last of the men moved into camp?" he demanded of his Quarg aide. The youth growled slightly before replying.

"All the Firthians and mercenaries, yes. We await only the Herthians, and we have word that they are near the tunnel."

"And what of your people?"

The youth respected and feared the Were; he was one of the few of his people that really understood what he was. That he could change into a wolf they understood, some of their own shamans could shape change, but not the magical side of the Curse that allowed only magical or silver weapons to kill them. He was also smart enough to know that withholding information was the one thing this man wouldn't tolerate.

"More come in every day, but others leave so you won't know how many are here. They continue to search for the Keon-din, and are loathe to give up the chase."

Cursing Handrick unconsciously bared his teeth; he needed the Quargs; all he could get his hands on, but as a race they were obsessed with catching this one man.

"One man; one man who cannot speak, is holding up the entirety of the Quarg warriors?" he snarled, swiping an imaginary claw at a nearby tree and nearly changing in his anger.

"He is the Keon-din," the youth stated, shrugging his shoulder. "He is an ancient enemy of our people."

"A man, a human man, who can not be more than three or four decades old," Handick stated, walking a few steps away. "How 'ancient' an enemy can he be? And one created by your people, if what I've heard is correct," he scoffed, continuing back on his path. "I understand the joy of playing with your prey; even torture has its place. But your people couldn't even finish the job when they had his throat all but ripped out?"

"He is the Keon-din," the youth repeated weakly, his arms waving ineffectually, then more strongly added, "he is a spirit warrior, and has great powers."

"He's a man, nothing more. A fine woodsman, undoubtedly, but still a man all the same. Will it take his death before your people will fully cooperate?"

Struggling with the human language, the youth had to concentrate in order to decide what, exactly, Handrick had meant.

"More warriors would come to follow you, if you killed the Keon-din," he stated, still unsure.

"Fine then, go and fetch Darington. Tell him to meet me here," Handrick ordered, stopping to stand in the shade of a massive tree.

Watching the youth run off, Handrick looked in grim humor on the tree. Someone had been using it for target practice, and most of the bark on the lower bole was missing. A few errant arrows could be seen further up still wedged into the wood. Apparently no one had wanted to climb up after them.

His wait was short; Darington was usually easy to find; that was one of the reasons Handrick asked for him. The other was that the man was the most vicious of all the Weres. A full head taller than Handrick, the man had been handsome before the Curse had altered his features. Powerful, he was the most youthful of the Weres in both age and time carrying the Curse and more than a little reckless. In other words he was perfect for what Handrick had in mind.

"You wanted me," the man grunted, his voice deep and guttural. So thoroughly had the Curse taken hold that the man had hair growing on his upper cheek bones and even his forehead. Of all the Weres under Handrick's command, he was the most dangerous.

"Yes, I have a task for you."

"Maybe I don't want a task," the man grunted, eyes narrowing. Darington never wanted to cooperate.

"You will do as you're told," Handrick growled, his hand drifting to his chest. Pleased he watched the bigger Were's eyes widen slightly at the movement.

"What do you want of me?" Darington growled, as close to surrender as he was likely to offer.

Careful to only smile with his lips, baring his teeth even slightly might have triggered the change in the uneasy Darington, Handrick explained what he needed.

"You want me to hunt down one man? I have to run through the forest for days on end looking for one normal human with no magic weapons or silver? This is beneath me, Handrick."

"You will be in command of a number of Quargs and as many wolves as you would like to lead. Run this man to ground and return to me; do it within two weeks and the attack of Aldrigal will be ready to move forward. Without his death we will continue to have less than the full cooperation of the Quargs."

"And if I don't?"

Again Handrick said nothing, merely raised his hand to his chest. He enjoyed the look of fear in the other Were's eyes. The surrender was sweet.

"Don't feel so bad, Darington. You're likely to make a lot of friends among the Quargs when you bring this fellow's head back. Set up some sort of trap in the foothills; back the man up against a cliff he can't climb or tunnel through and bury him under Quargs. They can do all the hard work for you."

Darington growled. "If I'm going to all this trouble I'm going to kill the man myself, and eat his heart in the bargain."

Chapter Twenty

Gran was happy that they had managed to slip out of the city unobserved. Or at least they were unobserved by anyone looking particularly for her. The carriage was so wide that some streets had to be avoided entirely while others were so choked with humanity that they could not pass easily through the crowd. The Viscount and his wife had been very well observed; she by imperiously ordering the way cleared for their carriage and he by his simple aloofness. Where she was hiring ruffians to physically remove anyone in the street, he was tossing small coins to the ground behind the wagon to accomplish the same thing. Both were effective at allowing some measure of progress as well as being seen, and remembered, by everyone they passed.

The carriage of the Viscount was elaborate to say the least. Every edge was gilded and even the wood used to build it had been imported from somewhere so far away that Gran wasn't familiar with it. However she did notice that the gilding was not exactly gold and the inlaid gems that encrusted the wheels were highly polished but were really quite common. Either the Viscount wished to be thought wealthier than he was or he did not want to reward the common thieves that likely stole the gemstones during his travels. Several were already missing. Perhaps they even fell out when the carriage hit holes in the road.

Inside the carriage was filled with cushions. Both bench seats, one to the front and another across the rear, were long enough and wide enough to really be classified as beds in Gran's mind. Even the floors were soft with piles of cushions all over a thick padding covered with soft linen. The Viscountess required all who entered to remove their footwear to avoid damage. Once the carriage was in motion the elf was friendly and talkative, spending her hours playing on a small harp and singing to herself or her husband. Lord Jamus drank heavily, particularly in the evenings, and slept as much as he could. He explained that he abhorred travel.

For three days after leaving Aldrigal Gran hid within the carriage before she dared to step outside. Doing nothing for so long had nearly driven her mad and in self defense against the crushing boredom she had cleaned the inside of the poor carriage until the Viscount begged her to stop before she "rubbed holes through the walls". The simpering Viscount's drinking and whining didn't help Gran's disposition any more than the fact that he wore more perfume than did his wife and thickened the air to the point that Gran found trouble drawing a good breath at times. She often declared, and quite loudly as well, that she was on the verge of dying from the unholy blend of scents. To Gran's mind the only good side of the whole trip was the time she and the elf had to talk.

One afternoon as Lord Jamus slept off the previous night's revels Gran and the elf, who insisted that Gran call her Eldena in private, sat together swapping stories of drunkard husbands. Gran had more tales but Eldena's were just as humorous and the two laughed until their sides hurt.

Sipping from a mug of water Gran suddenly turned the conversation serious.

"Why are you helping me, Eldena?"

Spoken so bluntly, the words surprised Eldena and she had to take a moment to gather her thoughts.

"Kelendle asked me to," she said, looking Gran in the eye.

"Yes, Kelendle asked you, he told me that, but why did you accept? Surely doing a favor for an innkeeper is not worth the danger of transporting a known felon?"

The elf smiled. "Perhaps not of its own merit but there are other factors to consider."

"Such as?"

"Such as the fact that Kelendle is more than just an innkeeper; he and my husband have been friends since childhood. They've been partners in many an escapade, on that you may trust me."

"What sorts of escapades?" Gran asked, never one to trust anyone's word on much of anything. Even when she did, she still hedged her bets.

"Oh, the usual things," laughed Eldena. "The usual things that two university students can find to do when one is a nobleman of adequate resources and the other a street-wise native of the area. Particularly when they share a common taste for women and wine and find themselves alone and unsupervised in a big city."

"Ah," snorted Gran. "Typical male foolishness."

"I know some females who managed a little foolishness in their time."

"When were you watching me?" demanded Gran in mock seriousness.

The two shared a quiet laugh punctuated by a groan from Jamus.

"But you aren't helping me because of an old drinking buddy of your husband's," Gran stated, speaking slightly louder than necessary in order to coax another groan from the man. She knew that she wouldn't intimidate the elf with her unblinking gaze but she tried it anyway.

Eldena looked away first. Certainly she wasn't intimidated by Gran but the elf felt a strange kinship with this old human.

"No, not entirely. I mean, that's why Jamus agreed to it, just because Kelendle asked him to. That's enough for him to agree to just about anything that doesn't force him to dirty his own hands, and I might have done it just because my husband asked me to…"

"That's not what I asked."

The elf nodded. "I know, Gran. You asked why I agreed to take you. Let's just say that I heard rumors about the Were attack and I know certain things about certain people," she said, then paused before continuing. "My, didn't that sound suitably cryptic! Let me try again."

"I wish you would," Gran said, scratching her head and feigning incomprehension.

Eldena leaned back against a pile of cushions and smiled. "I heard about the Were attack and that nearly everyone from two villages had been killed."

"True enough. One was wiped out almost completely and Cobble, the town I lived in, had only a few survivors," Gran agreed.

"Well, I also heard about the person you were said to have murdered. I met her once not so long ago. She said that she was a Were hunter and when she died I knew that you either had nothing to do with it or someone you loved had taken the Curse from that Were attack."

Gran was chagrined to hear that. She had hoped that it wouldn't be quite so easy for anyone to learn of Albrim's survival.

"Well don't lose any sleep over wondering if I really killed the woman or not; because I did. I poisoned her and hid the body," Gran stated in a matter of fact tone, daring the elf to condemn her for her actions. Spoken proudly too, or so Eldena believed.

"So someone did take the curse. I'm sorry Gran."

Gran waved the sympathy away. "What's done is done and he's taken care of now. No one will ever harm him, you can count on that. No one will ever even see him again, not in these parts."

"Yes, but will he harm any one else?" Eldena asked. Though her voice was quiet her words were clear. It was an awful risk to allow a Were to survive, even if it was someone you loved.

"No," stated Gran so strongly that Eldena started. The glare in the old woman's eye was sharp and confrontational. "He's been well taken care of. There are some who know what to do with a Were. They needn't all become mindless animals!"

"Of course not, Gran. There are stories of some who managed to build a productive life for themselves after becoming Cursed, but they are few. If you say that you knew what you were doing, then I believe you."

"Well I did and I still do, so that settles it," Gran huffed, changing the subject. "How did you know the woman that I poisoned?"

Eldena rolled her eyes when she thought Gran wasn't looking. "I met her on one of our travels. Jamus enjoys his leisure time so we pretty much do nothing but wander around and attend parties. I met her at the wedding of the Duke and Duchess of Firth a year or so back. She was a guard in the duke's castle. A very unpleasant woman as I recall, but she didn't act like a guard."

"So you're not thinking of revenging her death?"

Smirking Eldena replied. "I only remember her because I didn't like her very much. She was rude, loud, and obnoxious. Once I found out who she really worked for, I made sure not to talk to her anymore."

"Sounds like the same woman all right. She just wouldn't accept that my grandson was dead. Kept poking around, asking the same tired questions of the same people over and over. My neighbors heard her accusations so often that some of them began to believe her."

"I know the type."

Gran sipped again from her mug before asking. "Who exactly did the woman 'really' work for?"

Eldena knew that Gran was searching for information without trying to be too rude or obvious. Gran was not good at that. She was more the type of person who just demanded to know what she wanted. The elf accepted the effort as a compliment. Gran liked her well enough not to try and force information out of her.

"First of all Gran let me say that I'm not entirely comfortable sharing this type of information. It's the sort of innuendo that rich people like to hire assassins to quell, if you know what I mean. The woman worked for the Duke of Firth all right, but she wasn't normally a castle guard. She was one of the 'Brukahl', a fancy name for some bullies employed by the Duke of Firth. They're something like spies, but more like assassins in my opinion."

"So why would an assassin, or even a spy for that matter, be searching a back-water like Cobble for Weres? That doesn't make any sense."

"I agree, to a point, except the Duke of Firth is rumored to have more than a passing interest in Weres. Rumors are that he funds groups to hunt down anyone with the Curse. These Brukahl are believed to be the groups he sends."

"So the woman I killed wasn't alone?" Gran scoffed. "If there had been more of them, I would have known. She was alone, like as not."

"I'm not doubting you, Gran. Jarma was likely alone; she was probably sent ahead to scout around, but there will be others following her. I have no idea how many. Now that she's missing they may send an assassin or even a whole group of them to find out why, or just another scout. If they believe that there is a Were in this area, they will go to any lengths to take them."

"So the Duke of Firth sends people after those with the Curse?" Gran asked. "Why? Does he have a particular fear or hatred of Weres?"

"I have no idea as to why he does it, but he does. Duke Lionel von Firth has no altruistic or philanthropic sides, so it's not like he just wants to protect people. None of his family members died at the hands of a Were, at least not that I can discover. Whatever his reasons he does do it, though he has gone to some lengths to keep that a secret. Only someone with my abilities," she waggled her fingers for emphasis, "could hope to know even this much."

Gran chuckled. "I envy you those abilities. Where did you learn how to read someone's mind like that, much less be able to communicate with them. I liked to jumped out of my dress when you did it to me!"

They shared a laugh. Eldena taking Gran's words as nothing more than a jest, doubting that the older woman had ever been surprised by anything in her long life. Gran didn't bother to explain it; she was just glad she had been alone in her room when the elf used her magic to speak with her; Gran had jumped a good foot from the ground. Just then she remembered something Eldena had said earlier.

"When you were talking about the Brukahl, you said that the groups sent after the Weres 'take' them. Don't you mean kill them?"

"Not necessarily, no. Rumors say that the Brukahl sometimes try to take the Weres alive; particularly ones who haven't had the Curse very long and may not even be showing any of the signs, yet. I'm told it is for certain 'research' that they fund. Supposedly they work for a cure, but I doubt it. Other rumors say that the Weres they take alive die horrible deaths, eventually. If they're looking for a cure, they are going about it in a very strange manner. More likely they're looking for new and better ways of killing them."

"That will not happen to my grandson. These assassins will never even find him. Not where I put him, at least!"

"I'm pleased to hear it, Gran. I hope you're right about him. I hope that he never suffers from the Curse and is able to live a long and happy life despite it."

Gran slowly shook her head. "Long and happy has nothing to do with it. The boy will never have children; he'll never be able to live in one place for long unless it's away in the middle of nowhere. He'll be a wanderer, like as not, and make his living by the sword. Or worse, one of those silly rangers that live in the wilderness and supposedly 'protect' us from the raids of the Quargs and the like!" she sniffed. "More foolishness; the world is full of fools!"

"I can't argue that point, it's lined my pockets often enough."

"You're not born to the nobility, are you? You've the act down well enough, but I can see now that you don't look down on the peasantry enough to be real."

"Oh yes, but elven nobility titles rarely entail a great deal of monetary wealth, and we don't have a peasant class in Skallist. It's more of an honorary thing; to tell others that we descend from a notable or famous person. Elves love their history and knowing that I am a descendent of Hiala the Singer can be important in elven circles. Before I met Jamus, I was forced to earn my supper and I wasn't always scrupulous about where that supper came from. I dabble a little in magic," she confessed. "Mostly in the type that allows me to gain information. I never truly apprenticed to a master of the art but I had an aunt who did and she helped me a great deal. I have a knack for informational magic. I can't really read people's minds but I can determine certain... moods and important thoughts; mostly memories. It has come in handy on a number of occasions."

Gran allowed the conversation to die away for a moment and then returned to her original question. "So tell me, why did you agree to help me?"

Eldena had to marvel at the mind of this woman. She was impossible to lie to. "Gran, I have an interest in rare things. I enjoy the risk, the adventure of finding things lost to civilization. The thrill of risking everything, even my own life, to get them back."

Showing her disdain with a loud sniff, Gran made her opinion clear. "I don't think much of adventurers and I don't believe that's what you are. Not entirely."

Now it was Eldena's turn to change the subject, if Gran would let her. "Gran I am your friend. I will help you in your quest; that should be enough for now. Your enemies are my enemies."

Not liking it one bit Gran relented. Looking around the carriage she thought about what she could clean next. The dust from the draft animals was forever coming in the windows and coating everything. Her thoughts were distracted when the Viscount snored.

"You would do well to be rid of that one," she said, nodding towards Jamus.

"He's not really so bad, you know," the elf said, smiling fondly at the inebriated human. "I know what you see but that's just on the surface. A drunkard, a lay-about, a rich and spoiled brat. He's much more than that, at least to me."

"Love will often blind even those of a straight mind," Gran quoted. "Anyone devoted to a life of drinking and traveling is giving nothing back! Accomplishing nothing and helping no one."

"True in some ways, I suspect, but I love him Gran. He has an inner strength that I lack and a love for me that is true and pure. He completes me, Gran, as no other man ever has," she blushed. "Most people believe that I married him only for his money. That is an attractive 'extra', I will admit, but I married my Jamus out of love."

Gran snorted, "I loved a man once, and he up and died just when he was starting to become worth my efforts! He did give me children, however, and that is something you and Jamus cannot have. Why would either of you accept a marriage where children are not an option? Do you not need an heir? Surely Jamus does. Most human nobles trace their lineage exclusively through the men."

Eldena's blush deepened. "Gran it is true that we can never have children but our need for heirs is not great. I am not the eldest of my family nor even in the top three. Jamus is the eldest but he has several younger brothers and some of them already have children. The line of Gelbow is safe for at least one more generation."

"And the Lord of Gelbow is not needed to manage his estates?" Gran scoffed.

"No, Gran. The brothers as well as a few uncles manage fine without him. In truth they all have better minds for business than does my Jamus. All are honorable men too, good and honest. They make a good living for the entire family and Jamus is allowed to live his life pursuing his pleasures. It is a good arrangement for all of us."

Another long pause was broken this time by Eldena. "There is another benefit to traveling around with Jamus. I do have the occasional opportunity to perform, like you and I did back at the Jackdog. In fact, I have different personalities that I use whenever we visit a different city! I keep notes on who I am when we first visit a place and return to that persona when we return there again."

"Whatever for?" demanded Gran.

"For fun! I'm an elf, Gran, remember? We are supposed to be flighty and vacuous! I can't let my audience down, can I?"

"Foolishness, girl. Nothing but more foolishness. I thought you were smarter than that!" Gran said.

Eldena cocked her head to one side. "We all have depth to our personalities, Gran. You have your secrets and I have mine. The real fact is that I enjoy my life and adore doing what I do. Jamus and I are happy and in love. What could be more important than that?"

Gran sniffed. "Give me a parchment, a pen, and three days or so to get started and I'll make you a list."

"Gran, you certainly are interesting."

"Interesting doesn't interest me. Give me 'old and the same' every time. Interesting gets people killed, like as not."

"What has your life been like for you to feel that way?" wondered Eldena aloud.

"It's been spent working, as it should be; caring for children and hoeing cabbages," Gran replied, abruptly changing the subject again. "Tell me about the driver; can he be trusted?"

"Conn? Oh certainly. He's been with Jamus since he was a boy, and his family has served the Gelbow's for generations. A fine man and an experienced soldier; he not only knows how to fight he also knows how to keep his mouth closed."

"I don't believe that for a moment; the first time he gets inside an alehouse he'll spill all he knows, like as not."

"Conn doesn't drink, Gran, at least never that I've seen."

"All men drink, and all men get drunk," Gran quoted an old saying. "And I've never known a man to upset that rule either."

"Why must you be so unhappy, Gran? Is it a requirement of your religion or something?"

"Religion? Hardly! My philosophy in life is to make sure that the children are fed and happy, Eldena. Adults have other things to worry about then being happy; like responsibility and keeping the children alive! You've never had children. I have and they are all dead now along with my husband. I suppose he made me happy somewhat, in an annoying sort of way, but those days are past. I suffered when my children died, more than anyone should ever have to, and now I live only to fulfill my responsibilities and that is all."

"And those responsibilities have now become only the life of your grandson? Is he all the family you have left?"

Gran huffed and turned her back on the elf but not quickly enough that Eldena missed the tears welling in her eyes.

"I don't want to talk about my grandson."

Honoring the request Eldena lay back against the cushions and stared up at the roof of the carriage. Soon the regular rhythm of her husband's snores lulled her off into a fitful sleep. She couldn't have slept more than a few moments at most; it seemed like no more, when she was awakened by a shout.

"Halt the carriage in the name of the Duke of Firth!"

Chapter Twenty-One

Dirk did not actually run through the hallways but the servants and other functionaries he passed darted from his path as if he were. Technically the servants were not even supposed to know that the man existed. They didn't know exactly who he was, but they knew he was someone the duke trusted and studiously avoided meeting his gaze as they stepped aside. Moving as quickly as he thought prudent the former assassin had sought the duke in his private chambers only to be told that he was in the baths. Ignoring the steam that poured from the door of his destination Dirk flung it open and darted into the obscuring mist calling for the duke.

Lionel recognized the excitement in Dirk's voice and emerged from a side room wrapped only in a towel. His skin fairly glowed from the scrubbing he had just endured, not to mention the attentions of the servant whose duty it was to remove the hair from his back, and his bare feet made wet slapping noises on the damp floor.

"In here, Dirk," the duke ordered, moving through another door to a smaller side room where they could speak in privacy as his attendants wisely fled. Lionel didn't know whether to be excited or angry with the man.

"What are you doing here," the duke hissed, keeping his voice down just in case someone lingered; spies in his home were not to be unexpected. "You're not supposed to enter the house during the day, you know that you fool! What if someone recognized you?"

Dirk bobbed his head in apology as he blurted, "I'm sorry, My Lord, but you said to come immediately when I received this. I thought perhaps it was too important to wait."

Intrigued the duke held his peace; Dirk was efficient and not prone to taking unwarranted risks, and arranging a meeting through the usual routes would most likely have delayed their speaking for hours. He'd have to do something about that.

"Let me see," Lionel said, excitement taking over despite himself. There were only a few things he could imagine that were important enough for Dirk to disobey a restriction he knew to be prudent. Whatever damage the man's appearance had caused was done; the time when his political enemies within Firth could harm him were soon to be past anyway.

From an inside pocket Dirk drew a single piece of parchment. It was new, folded in half, and had up to very recently been sealed with wax. The seal had only been broken along one corner, so most of the symbol impressed in it was still visible. Lionel's breath came short when he saw the tree and one shaking hand involuntarily went to his chest.

Opening it slowly, almost reverently, the duke enjoyed the moment. He knew that in the future he would remember this day, this instant, as the one when all his past struggles fell away and the day of his ascension began. He'd always had royal aspirations; believing that Firth deserved to be a kingdom and he a king. Today those beliefs were beginning to come true. Desperation from the loss of his mines combined with the subsequent draining of his treasury might have forced his hand but Lionel firmly believed that it would have happened regardless. The invasion of Aldrigal would confirm what he already knew.

The words were small and printed in a concise, neat hand. The first few lines were nothing more than formal greetings and then a confirmation of the presence of the king of Aldrigal at his summer palace. At the last were well wishes for him in the struggles to come, and a gentle reminder of his duties. It was the other part of the letter that held his gaze; three-quarters of the way down the page. His breath came rapidly as he lifted his gaze back to Dirk. The assassin knew then that he had not been wrong in his decision to come now.

"Send a rider to Handrick," the duke joyfully said, "tell him to begin the invasion."

Chapter Twenty-Two

To their left the cliff fell away; to go that direction was death. The woods to their right were filled with shouting Quargs and baying wolves and certainly represented no better. The ground where they ran was smooth stone and so was mostly clear of brush save an occasional hearty bush or blade of grass that managed to struggle for life in a crack or crevice. This left no cover for the two running men. The one, large, bearish, wearing furs and raw leather, ran stooped with a massive longbow in one hand. His smaller companion ran more upright, a smaller bow clutched in his left. The smaller man's right hand was missing; the stub encased in an odd-looking apparatus of steel bars that ended in a hook. Mute and Albrim were running for their lives.

Quargs began to emerge from the forest behind and before them and lined up their bows for what amounted to an easy shot despite the moving targets. Wolves of all sizes also entered the clear area from all along the tree line and shot towards their prey at full speed. A dozen arrows were fired, then two dozen as twice that many wolves drew near. Years of torment and death would be repaid this day; today the Keon-din would suffer for his crimes against the Quarg. Their revenge would finally be complete. Shouts of victory arose from the throats of the Quargs.

Shouts that became gasps of surprise when their quarry disappeared before their very eyes.

The spent arrows fell like rain upon the ground, striking nothing more than rock save for one overly enthusiastic and speedy wolf that yelped in surprise. As a pack the beasts gathered around the spot where they had last seen the men and then one by one sat upon their haunches and howled mournfully. Quargs, disbelieving their eyes, ran to the spot and kicked their way through the wolves to see if by chance the two humans were still there, their bodies filled with arrows within some unseen dip in the rock. All the hunters found besides their bent and broken arrows was a long crack in the ground, barely wide enough for a human to fit within and no more than waist deep; not large enough for the men to hide within or even get out of sight. Yet it was empty.

A few Quargs ran along the edges of the crevice, looking for some sign of the humans. Those that approached the edge of the cliff saw that the crevice fell away there, leaving a pathway down a chimney along the face of the cliff. Pushing and shoving they leaned down to see if their prey was within sight. A flash of movement convinced them that they were, and so the quickest of the Quargs leaped down into the crevice and prepared to climb down the chimney to continue the pursuit and took an arrow in his throat for his troubles. Below came a hoot of laughter as Albrim taunted the Quargs.

"Come on down, we're ready for you! Plenty more arrows where those came from!" he shouted.

"What did he say?" demanded a Quarg. None of those clustered about the crevice spoke any language but their own. All recognized a taunt, however, and knew that the Keon-din was inviting them to enter this crevice and die like the first Quarg.

Again the Quargs began pushing and shoving, but this time it was to force others into the chimney ahead of them. One warrior slipped from the cliff and fell to his death in the struggle but eventually one of the smaller Quargs was forced into the opening. When no further arrows appeared the warriors cautiously began descending after the humans.

Three body lengths down the chimney ended and a dark hole was found. Another trap prepared in advance by Mute, a thick springy branch bent to its maximum, was triggered and the first Quarg into the opening was flung off the cliff face. No further arrows came from the darkness but fear of the Keon-din had replaced the bloodlust and none of the Quargs would be the first into the dark hole. Arguing among themselves the warriors decided that there was no way that they could bring the wolves down here quickly enough to lead the pursuit, so they sat clustered about the crevasse until a Were arrived to take command and forced the warriors into the cave.

The descent was long and dark and within the small cave the Quargs found that Mute had more traps ready to cover his back trail. More of their warriors died as the tunnel dropped steeply and steadily downward into the rock of the cliff. Afraid of the Were and the retribution they would face the Quargs moved as cautiously as they dared down into the cave; nominally in pursuit of the humans but none of them had any expectations of catching up to the pair. The legends grew ever greater that day.

The Keon-din had escaped again.

Chapter Twenty-Three

"Darington is dead? A mute woodsman and a boy, neither of which had magic or silver, killed a Were?" demanded Handrick.

The Quarg trembled. It was not unknown among his people for leaders to kill those delivering bad news.

"Yes sir, a runner just came," the aide squeaked, saliva slipping unheeded down his chin. "His head was crushed by a log, and then somebody cut if off..."

"Crushed by a log! The fool hadn't even changed," the Were roared, kicking a camp chair aside in disgust. "That's two of us that have died on this side of the mountains, two," he thundered, holding up the appropriate digits to the other Weres gathered with him.

"He was young and reckless," offered one.

"He might have just been surprised," argued a second. "It might have happened to any of us; we're not immortal."

"Stupid, that's what he was," stated Mol, the oldest of them in age if not years while Cursed. "He's not the first young man to believe that bad things can only happen to someone else."

Handrick waved them all to silence. Each were right, or could be, in their own way but he needed time to think. The loss of Darington was not the worst that could come out of this mess.

"Which way did they go?"

"East and a little south," the Quarg answered. "Our trackers have a cordon in place and are in pursuit; they're driving the Keon-din ahead and not allowing him to circle back around to his home area. Our chiefs feel that if he does that he will again disappear into the shadow world."

"Fools, this is his home area! If he came back here he'd walk right into our hands," growled a Were.

"And by driving him southeast he will eventually stumble across a settlement and warn of our presence," added Handrick. "All it would take is one and Aldrigal would be alerted and waiting for us with their armies."

"What can we do? If the Quargs can't catch him, there's no way we can," asked Mol. "Whatever damage done there is already done."

"Not to mention that there no settlements that way; it's practically on the border of Aldrigal and there's nothing between there and Skallist," offered another. "What can he do? Warn a merchant caravan to turn back? Nothing that will stop our invasion; provided it happens soon."

"And that should be any day," said another Were, his thick red beard the only one of that color in the group other than their leader. "What's the word from Firth, Handrick?"

"Nothing new," Handrick growled, stalking about the tent like the wolf he was. "I'm expecting the regular dispatch rider any moment."

As if by prophecy the sound of hoof beats came to the keen-eared Weres at that moment. Leading them outside, Handrick shaded his eyes as he stared up the mountain road. Seconds later a hard-riding horse came into view through the trees, his horse's breath steaming in the frigid air.

"He's riding awfully fast," commented Mol.

"Faster than normal," added Warren; the newest Were to join them now that Darington was dead.

"Something's up," added another, though Handrick didn't look around to see who had spoken; his attention was focused on the rider; the man was indeed pushing his steed. Stepping out from the others, the Were held up his hand until the courier caught sight of him and guided his mount to them.

"My Lord," the man gasped, handing down a single thin envelope to Handrick rather than the thick stack of dispatches he normally received. The excitement he smelled on the rider told him all he needed to know; opening the envelope was merely a formality. Tearing through the thin paper he glanced once at the hastily scrawled words. The proper form had been followed; the orders were legitimate.

Handrick looked to his Quarg aid, grabbing the youth by the arm in ensure his attention. "Send riders, not Quargs on foot, to catch up to your people who are chasing the woodsman. Order them to close the Skallist road and beginning sweeping up the settlements in that area while they chase their ghost. Order the Quargs here to march straight through to the king's palace, just like we planned, and send a rider back to gather up anyone not in camp and get them organized."

"Its come hasn't it," Mol growled, delight clearly written on his face.

"Just like we planned, my brothers," Handrick snarled, his canines prominently displayed. "Gather the troops; we march."

Chapter Twenty-Four

Dawn of the fourth day after their escape from the cliffs found Mute and Albrim running along a trail many miles away. The lead they had gained in the caves had given them a head start but the Quargs and wolves were numerous and doggedly kept up the pursuit.

Albrim knew that they were nearing the edge of the range Mute normally patrolled and soon would be forced to leave behind the stashes of food and equipment he kept and regularly replenished. However the Quargs in pursuit were not allowing him the opportunity to circle back as they had in the past and had even begun searching the treetops more carefully as well, barring the humans' use of the trees as a road to double back.

Never had Mute seen so many wolves. His stock of natural scents was nearly gone and that had taken years to stockpile. As much as possible he and Albrim slept off the ground and even traveled that way when the trees were large enough and grew close enough together. Every stream they passed became a highway as Mute sought to lose their scent in the water. This would help them avoid or lose one set of wolves but eventually they would have to leave the stream and another pack would soon pick them up again. Both men were near to exhaustion and almost out of tricks.

Almost but not quite. Mute had a few ideas left.

Not so far away lay the main road that ran between Aldragal in the north and Skallist to the south. A major highway that was wide and well patrolled for some distance out of both nations. Some parts were even partially paved and the ruts were filled every three or four years when the King of Aldragal had enough prisoners built up to perform the labor. Mute believed that if they could reach the highway they could follow along it for miles; losing their pursuit once and for all. No wolf could follow their scent among the many others that daily used that road. At least Mute didn't think so.

Not to mention the regular patrols. Mute hoped that the Quargs would be unwilling to approach the highway and so reveal their presence. Even if they did intend invasion, and the presence of smoke to the north made Mute suspicious that they were already doing that, they would not want to expose themselves too soon. If the Quargs cared not, then surely the Weres would. Either way the highway should free them of pursuit and they might even pick up a ride with a merchant caravan. Mute had done so from time to time without being discovered despite the many wanted posters with his likeness placed along the highway. A strong guard with his own bow was a fine addition to a caravan along the highway as it was not unheard of for bandits to plague the area in years that the Quargs did not. Not to mention the wild creatures that filled the forests this far south.

By Royal Decree the land along the highway had been cleared back the distance of a bow shot. The area actually cleared had never reached that distance nor had it ever been properly maintained, yet the trees were cut about every ten years and the brush could only grow so high. This left plenty of ambush points for bandits and patrols looking for bandits and also allowed Mute to get within the length of a sword to the highway without being seen. There he and Albrim waited, resting and sharing a bit of food while listening for sounds of pursuit or travelers along the highway. For a long time they heard neither.

Albrim lay back in the cool grass and allowed the sunshine to soak into his skin. He was glad to feel its warmth and to smell the scent of a nearby bush; it was past harvest time but the weather remained humid. The last time he had glimpsed the mountains it had looked to be snowing there, so it wouldn't be too much longer before winter came to the lowlands but today, at least, the weather remained warm during the day despite the early morning frosts. Much of the time when living in the deep forest they suffered the heat of the sun without actually seeing the golden orb itself. It felt so good that he longed to just let himself go and sleep right there. Surely they were safe here, weren't they? The sun passed overhead and Albrim did indeed sleep. Mute left him and took a quick scout around the area. No Quargs were within sight or sound but he didn't place any confidence in either. He had been taken unaware by the force that had ambushed him on the cliff top and only years of caution had led him to scout out a quick escape route when he chose the place for his ambush. Mute was good in the forest, he knew that because he was still alive after all these years, but he also knew that no one was perfect.

Returning to find his friend still asleep Mute sat with him for a time, seeking his own rest as much as he could while remaining awake. He passed the time counting the passing travelers, which were few this far from Aldragal, watching wagon loads of produce and single merchants leading lines of mules or pack horses bearing their wears one direction or the other. To the north flowed fruits and tanned hides along with dyes and pigments from Skallist. To the south went baskets of grain and fish from the rivers of Aldragal. Local farmers moved their wares to the nearest village markets on two wheeled carts that always amazed Mute. He didn't see why they didn't tip over whenever the donkeys that pulled them stopped. If any of the travelers were concerned about the smoke they didn't show it. After all, it was well back off the road and so was likely nothing but another forest fire. Nothing passed that Mute cared to travel with. It was important to join a large caravan with a number of guards. That way the merchant would be more concerned with defending his rich cargo and less likely to ask questions or look too closely at those defending it. Albrim was too easily marked and remembered with the hook contraption replacing his missing hand but Mute wasn't too concerned about the boy being recognized. Mute however was infamous along the highway from the years of wanted posters. His size and the scars on his neck made him impossible to miss when he did not have the time to disguise himself properly.

Darkness would fall in another hour so Mute awoke Albrim and
motioned for him to rise. They would follow the road south for a while and
watch for a caravan. Meeting one or allowing it to catch up to them did not
matter but it was time they were moving. Whether the Quargs were
minutes behind or hours Mute couldn't know, but he suspected the former
more than the latter, though he was somewhat reassured by the sounds of
the forest. If Quargs were about in any numbers, particularly when
accompanied by wolves, the birds would go silent. The sounds of hoof beats
caused Mute to feel a moment's concern, why he couldn't have said but he
trusted his instincts, so he held up his hand, warning Albrim to stay
hidden. From the north he saw a fancy carriage approaching and a lone
horseman spurring his mount to pass or overtake it.

Curious and wary Mute decided to see what was happening before
leaving their shelter. The lone rider did not seem to be with the carriage
and might be the point man for a group of bandits. The driver seemed
unconcerned, however, and did not spare the rider a glance as he swept
past. This changed quickly when the rider stopped his horse in the road,
forcing the driver to pull up his teams.

"Halt that wagon in the name of the Duke of Firth!" the rider shouted,
brandishing a sword that shined brightly in the last rays of the sinking sun.
The fellow was well-armed; besides the sword he had a both a rapier and a
dagger on his belt and what looked like a hunting bow hanging from his
saddle. His clothing was dusty but appeared to be new; with boots so
polished they might never have caressed the bare earth.

The driver did nothing once the horses were stopped, simply sitting on
the seat and returning the horseman's stare. Finally he broke the silence.

"You'll move yourself, My Lord, or I'll run you down," Conn shouted,
snapping the reins and then immediately pulling the horses back. "If you're
looking for an easy robbery you should look elsewhere. There are no easy
pickings here," he added, looking confident but his voice betrayed his
nervousness. There might be a dozen armed men hiding in the carriage to
back him up but there could be a hundred times as many concealed within
the woods.

"If you move those horses again, I shall slay the lead beast and then
you," snarled the horseman, urging his mount up alongside the nearest
draft horse. The placid animal didn't even shy away as blinders left him
oblivious to both the approach of the other horse or the raised weapon and
the breeze was still wrong to bring the scent of the rider.

Calmly, almost regretfully, the driver put down the reins and lifted a
crossbow from the floor by his feet. The weapon was already cocked and a
quarrel was pulled from somewhere out of Mute's sight and purposefully
loaded.

"My Lord," the driver shouted, somewhat overly loud to Mute's mind,
as if he were really warning someone inside the carriage even as he
addressed the horseman. Surely those within knew what was going on. "If
you harm that horse it'll be your own mount that takes its place, after I spit
you on this bolt."

If the horseman was intimidated he did not show it. In fact Mute found
himself admiring both men's bravery. Both were open and exposed, not
knowing if the other was alone or perhaps had hidden allies. The value of

the carriage hinted at an occupant with wealth who could afford to buy war wizards as easily as carriages. The horseman could be the lead representative to a whole band of brigands. Somehow Mute doubted that either man had any support at all but you'd never know that by their attitudes. Brave didn't mean foolish, but the two could often be confused.

Silently Mute and Albrim worked their way through the underbrush towards the carriage and so missed the next verbal exchange between the men on the road. Mute wished that he and Albrim could somehow cross the highway without being seen so as to be behind the lone horseman but it was too bright for that. Stringing his bow and motioning for Albrim to do the same, Mute settled into the new spot to better observe what was happening on the road; he found that he was very interested in the standoff.

"Driver what is the hold up?" shouted a woman's voice from the carriage.

Mute glanced towards the door but saw no one as the windows he could see were covered with heavy draperies. Likely the woman had opened a door on the far side or perhaps used a window. Either way Mute could not find a face to put with the voice. It was pretty, almost musical, and reminding him of an elven voice. But this was not an elven carriage.

"My Lady we have a difficulty here," stated the driver, his voice absolutely calm as he kept his eyes on the horseman. "A brigand is threatening to kill one of the horses, please remain within the carriage until the matter is dealt with."

"I am no brigand!" shouted the horseman, the anger in his voice relaying his wounded pride. "I am an agent of the Duke of Firth, no common backwoods thief!"

"We are friends of the Duke of Firth, my good man, and so back away and allow us to continue," came the thin nasally voice of a man from within the carriage.

"You will disembark the carriage immediately," stated the horseman, lifting his voice so that all could hear.

The driver sighted along the bolt. "My Lord, step away from there and sheath your sword, I won't warn you again."

"Be gone, my good man, we have no issues with the Duke of Firth," shouted the man from within the carriage. "A right honorable fellow he is, a congenial and conscientious host."

"Step down from the carriage or face the wrath of Firth!" yelled the horseman.

"Step away or die!" yelled the driver.

"Wait, Conn, wait," ordered the male voice. "We have nothing to fear from our good friend the Duke of Firth or those who serve him. Hold thy blade, my good fellow, both my lady wife and I shall step down. Give us but a moment to regain our clothing."

Cruelly spurring his mount, the horseman rode to the side of the carriage beyond Mute and Albrim's sight. He shouted something unintelligible and the female voice they heard earlier screamed an oath in protest. The driver leapt to his feet and stepped atop the carriage and despite his Lord's order kept his weapon trained on the horseman.

"My Lord, give me your leave!" shouted the driver.

"Relax, Conn, there will be no trouble here. We shall step down," the man inside said before his voice faded away into something Mute couldn't make out.

The far carriage door slammed open and a pair of small feet in green leather slippers stepped to the ground. Speaking quickly the woman's voice was putting together a stream of insults and curses that made little sense other than to express her anger. Finally she calmed herself enough to string together a complete sentence.

"The Duke of Firth shall hear of this outrage!" she promised.

If the horseman heard her he did not bother to respond.

"Step out of the carriage, you," he snarled, apparently speaking to the man with the nasally voice unless there was someone else in the carriage. "Step down now or I will kill this elf!"

"Now see here," whined the man as his bare feet joined those of the elf on the trail. "You cannot threaten me! I am the Viscount of Gelbow and shall not be spoken to in such a manner!" he added, his tone all but groveling.

"Your leave, My Lord, please!" demanded the driver, the crossbow unwavering.

"No, Conn!"

"I said everyone, out of the carriage now!" shouted the horseman, the anger in his voice sending an unaccountable shiver of fear down Albrim's spine.

"Shouldn't we move closer?" he whispered to Mute. "We can't do anything from here. We should at least cross the road."

Mute shrugged, then led the way from the brush and out onto the highway. This late in the evening most of the traffic along the road had already stopped for the night so the highway remained empty in both directions. Only the driver of the carriage among those that participated in the macabre play was in a position to see them and his attention was riveted upon the horseman. Only Albrim and Mute could see the carriage door on their side quietly open and a figure slipping out. By the awkwardness of the movements the person was obviously elderly and no threat to anyone that he could see so Mute promptly ignored the figure.

"There is no one else in the carriage," shouted the elf.

"Lying elf," snarled the horseman, followed by the sound of a weapon upon flesh.

"NO!" screamed the Viscount, his scream of anguish echoed by the driver as the second man fired his quarrel.

Mute broke into a run, Albrim close behind him. The larger man didn't see the smaller stop abruptly in the middle of the road as he stared in disbelief at the person leaving the carriage. She was a small person, stooped as if aged, wearing a long gray cloak and clutching a walking staff. A whisp of gray hair blew from beneath the hood and a furtive glance in his direction told Albrim all he needed to know, even if he couldn't comprehend just how it had come about.

It was Gran!

Chapter Twenty-Five

Mute was surprised at the speed with which the next events occurred. He himself had just ran around the lead horses of the carriage in time to see a small figure, either a woman or a child, stumble to the side and then crumple to the ground, a shrieking man dressed in what appeared to be a green silk bathrobe only a moment behind as he dived protectively atop her. The bolt fired by the driver immediately after the horseman's strike had driven deeply into the chest of the horseman, driving him back in the saddle but amazingly not throwing him to the ground. Smiling, the man shrugged the blow off as inconsequential and seemed to flow rather than move to stand atop his saddle. The horseman was already in mid change and the form that easily leapt from the saddle to the top of the carriage was now human in basic form only.

His head was definitely wolf-like and his body sprouted fur even as he leaped, the horse beneath him standing steady as it had been trained. The driver managed a scream and dropped his crossbow before the Were was upon him but that was all; his feeble attempts to pull a knife were unsuccessful as he died where he stood. Ripping into the man with claws and teeth the Were literally tore the fellow to shreds, flinging handfuls of severed intestines to either side in his bloodlust. Finished with that threat the Were paused to tear the quarrel from its chest and toss it away. Nothing so ordinary as that could harm him once he had begun his change, though it had been painful. Throwing back his head the Were howled its joy at the killing, the heart-stopping bay of a carnivore that has killed and now plans to feed at its leisure. It did not pause but lifted a second howl on the heels of the first; looking down as it spied out its next victim.

Mute briefly considered launching an arrow from his massive bow but quickly realized the futility of the attack. Not only would it fail to do any damage to the Were it would turn the beast's attention on him. His mind was blank as the man tried to think of some way he and Albrim could escape the Were's clutches, along with the survivors from the carriage if possible. Mute decided that their only chance was if the Were paused to feed on the corpse of the driver, otherwise the beast could kill them all at his leisure. Even running was of no use if the Were chose to follow; Mute knew that he couldn't outrun the thing anymore than he could outrun a wolf, and he had no ready cave or other escape route prepared this time. Biding his time, the big man watched the Were closely while holding as still as he could; it was movement that would attract the Were's attention.

Burstis stalked to the edge of the carriage and looked down upon the woman he had attacked, as yet unaware of Mute standing just a short distance behind him. Burstis was angry; the cursed elf had attempted some type of magic on him, he'd felt the stirring in his mind, and he had reacted to protect himself. Wizard she might have been but one glance at the blood pouring from her scalp told him that she would not be a threat to him, not any longer. Turning his gaze to the man prostrated atop her, wailing as if it were his own blood pouring upon the ground, Burstis decided that her mate looked soft, flabby, not even a worthy meal. His meat would be thin and his blood weak. Burstis dismissed the man in an instant; he was armed, if only with a thin rapier belted around his dressing gown, but he was no warrior and certainly no real threat.

Almost Burstis recognized the Viscount of Gelbow, but not quite. The vaguely familiar face faded from the Were's memory within the fog of the Curse and the bloodlust that was upon him. This foppish noble would die, he must to prevent any knowledge of the attack from getting out, but he could wait. The fool was busy wailing over his mate and would likely still be there when Burstis returned for him. His true prey was nearby; Burstis could smell her.

Giving one last howl of victory simply for the sheer savage joy of it, Burstis turned away from the nobles to follow the spoor of the woman; Gran had to be nearby, likely trying to escape by the far side of the carriage or still cowering within it. Pausing to listen to his echo the Were was pleased to hear it return to him without being marred by any forest sounds; no birds, no crackling of brush; all was silent at his command.

For a few moments.

The victory howl of the Were was suddenly answered by a chorus of dozens more from the forest, which was in turn followed by the sounds of war horns and distant shouts. Quarg war horns. Dozens of Quarg war horns.

Expecting the Were to be pleased at the sounds of his allies' approach, Mute was amazed to see that the Were spun to look into the woods as if he too was surprised.

The shouts and war cries of hundreds of Quargs grew deafening as the humanoids descended upon the highway with their wolf allies. The Were's surprise lasted only a moment and then he moved into action, crossing the carriage and looking down for the person he had come to kill, then growling his pleasure at the sight of the old woman attempting to escape on that side. Gran was moving as swiftly as she was able, but the seconds bought by Conn's death had allowed her only a few steps towards safety; a safety that no longer was with the coming of the Quargs.

Mute wasn't sure what the Were was up to but once it left his line of sight he turned and ran back again to the other side of the carriage. There he found that the Were had jumped down from the vehicle and was standing astride a figure wearing a gray cloak that Mute recognized as the person he had seen leave the carriage. The beast-man must have leapt atop the person and forced them to the ground. Standing before the Were, no more than an arm's length away, was Albrim.

Chapter Twenty-Six

Seeing Gran was a shock more than a surprise for Albrim, as he had given up on ever seeing her or anyone from his old life again. For a long moment he simply stared, ignoring the shouts and screams from beyond the carriage, unwilling to move forward and find that it wasn't Gran but rather some figment of his imagination placing her features on the face of another elderly woman. She, whether Gran or not, didn't see him but moved as quickly as she was able for the trees across the road. Tears welled as he looked upon his grandmother; the whippings and switchings of his youth forgotten now; all Albrim remembered were the loving caresses and gentle voice he had enjoyed. His memory brought to him the scent of cookies and pies; along with the warm milk Gran often brought him just before bed.

Finally Albrim broke free from his reverie and took a few halting steps towards her, a smile on his face and her name about to be shouted in pleasure. Then his joy turned to horror as he saw Gran driven to the ground by a figure that had leapt from the carriage above. A figure that he knew very well as it wore a shape and form he had seen often in his nightmares over the last year and more.

Albrim gasped at the sight of the bestial Were and stopped there in the road before it, involuntarily reaching for his missing arm as the dull ache he often felt in his stump swelled to an agonizing burst of pain. Involuntarily Albrim staggered backwards, one foot falling into a rut and almost pitching him onto his back. Fears he had thought past and issues long dealt with surged to the forefront as he looked upon the Were, remembering that night when his arm had been taken and his life changed forever.

At first intent only on the victim he had come here to kill, the Were was distracted by the scent of this person who stood shaking in fear before him. The boy carried the Curse, of that the Were was immediately aware, but there was something else about him; something that simply smelled wrong. He was a Were but also smelled of silver, and was tainted by sorcery. This one would be a great find for Firth indeed.

Astonished that he had been so fortunate, the agent of Firth recognized in Albrim the Cursed he had been hunting Gran to find! As finding this one was his underlying mission, Gran no longer had any intelligence value to him. However she had killed an agent of the Brukahl and so she could not be allowed to live even if she wasn't a witness to his actions. Dirk, and through him the Duke of Firth, had been very explicit as to what Burstis was supposed to do with any witnesses.

Wary but intent upon his duty the Were growled once at Albrim, warning him away from the kill, before bending down to finish the old woman at his feet.

"Stay back boy, we'll talk once I finish here," he growled, his canine snout made it difficult to pronounce the words but Burstis had no doubt the youngster understood him. Crouching down over his prey, the Were moved to swiftly rip out the old woman's throat.

Only to feel the impact of an arrow that struck the side of his face. Stunned by the surprising force the Were was staggered but of course took no damage. The arrow was neither silver nor magical and so did not penetrate his Cursed skin despite the pain. However it did make the Were angry enough to forget the helpless prey before him and turn to evaluate this newest threat, catching only a glimpse of Mute standing by the horses before Albrim recovered from his surprise and lifted his own bow, firing at point blank range into the Were's chest and driving the creature back into the side of the carriage from the force of the blow. Again unharmed the Were snarled and leapt towards Albrim, expecting the young man to change shape and battle him Were to Were.

Albrim had no time to think and fell back from the attack out of reflex, managing to get his feet into the Were's chest, he rolled back onto his own shoulders and used the monster's own momentum to toss the beast over him. Mute had not been the first to teach him that maneuver as Borel, Albrim's father, had shown him several such wrestling techniques while growing up. Older boys had steered well clear of Albrim after only a couple of demonstrations.

Spinning about with amazing agility the Were landed on all fours facing the way he came and leaped again at the seemingly helpless Albrim who still lay on his back on the highway. Albrim responded by bringing his metallic arm across in a sweeping blow that caught the Were on the muzzle, staggering him again.

Hesitating before realizing that he was still unhurt, the Were dived at Albrim once more and again felt the hammering blow of an arrow fired by Mute's massive longbow, this time striking him on the temple. Snarling his rage the Cursed man turned toward Mute only to be startled again by the howls of wolves in the forest behind it. Not just wolves, there were likely Weres in that group as well. Weres loyal to Handrick who hated him and would not take kindly to his being here, except as an excuse to kill him.

But first he must deal with these insects. Kill the old woman and the big man and capture the young Were, then finish the nobleman beyond the carriage; that was his focus.

Chapter Twenty-Seven

Viscount Jamus was known in many lands as a gentleman and a philanthropist, prone to giving to the poor so long as he did not have to see them and donating lavishly to worthy causes. He was also a publicly avowed coward and twice had fled cities to avoid duels he could not purchase his way free of. He was known as a dandy and a darling of the social set but no one who knew him would call him a hero. He knelt in the dust of the highway and held his beloved wife in his arms, trying to avoid the sight of the horrible head wound she had suffered and instead gazed only upon her beautiful face.

She was too good for him, and he'd always known that. Their time together had been wonderful; every day something to look forward to. He'd never known true happiness until she had entered his life. Her family despised him as his had despised her. The difference was that his family had quickly changed their minds after meeting Eldena. His entire existence had changed direction because of her. And now she was gone.

Was his death soon to follow? Did he care to live on without his wife? Jamus trembled and wept. A coward would never let himself be killed even if he was afraid to live without his soul mate. No one would expect the Viscount of Gelbow to defeat a Were in combat nor even to know how, but he did know something about them. He knew that normal weapons were of no use; only a weapon of silver or magic could penetrate their tough hides. The Viscount might be a coward, but he was also wealthy and riches could purchase things such as enchanted weapons. An enchanted weapon such as the one he had belted on over his night robe when he had left the carriage.

Jamus gently lay his wife's shattered head upon the road and then drew the slender foil from its scabbard. Crawling to the carriage as his tears marked his trail, the Viscount collapsed beneath the vehicle in time to see a young man kick the Were over his prone body onto the road. Sick with remorse at the loss of his wife the Viscount ignored the rocking of the carriage wheels around him as the nervous horses prepared to bolt and tossed his foil to the young man's side. That task complete, Jamus crawled back to his wife; he couldn't bear to be away from her now.

Chapter Twenty-Eight

Mute fired another arrow into the Were as he sought to draw its attention away from Albrim. He knew that the younger man had nothing to fear from the Were's Curse but he also knew that Albrim would never be able to survive a fight with the creature hand to hand. Unable to change while wearing the magical armband that kept his Curse under control, Albrim would have no more chance to survive the Were's attack than would any other human. Mute took some heart at the indecisiveness of the Were; the creature couldn't seem to decide whether to finish off the boy, come after Mute, or attack the gray-cloaked figure. Then the Were seemed to make a choice just as Mute's next arrow ricocheted off the creature's arm.

Ignoring Mute, the Were seemed to be trying to reach the gray-robed figure that had collapsed in the road. That was something Albrim was trying to prevent as the younger man, utilizing the time bought him by Mute's arrow barrage, had now scrambled to his feet and moved to take a defensive stance over her. Taking aim again even as the Were leaped up and over the boy, Mute saw movement to his left at the edge of the road from the corner of his eye. Glancing that way Mute saw a Quarg standing there amidst the waist-high brush, aiming his own bow at Albrim. Shifting his attack Mute placed his missile through the Quarg's neck.

Again came the crashing crescendo of Quarg war horns, this time so close that the leaves seemed to shake from the sound, accompanied by the howls of hundreds of wolves. The brush at the edge of the road was moving in several places as one enemy after another approached the highway. In seconds they would be overwhelmed by a swarm of Quargs. Perhaps even more Weres.

Powerful Were jaws clamped down on Albrim's metallic arm. Desperately the young man had forced it there to avoid having his throat torn out. The claws of the Were were tearing at his chest as the two rolled over Gran's still form in their struggle. With his left hand Albrim tried to pull his belt knife but found only an empty scabbard, for all the good the puny weapon would have done him. Frantically he tried punching the Were but the beast never even noticed.

Only the awkwardness of his position, and the fact that Albrim kept rolling about to keep him off-balance, kept the Were from using his claws to disembowel the boy. Tired of trying to bite through steel and desperate to escape before the other Weres arrived, the agent of Firth released his bite and instead snapped at the one-armed boy's other arm.

Screaming at the thought of losing his remaining arm, Albrim tried to roll beneath the snapping jaws but to no avail as the Were bit down hard upon his upper arm, its teeth sinking quickly through the soft fabric and leather. Albrim continued to squirm; trying to pull his arm free, screaming for Mute to save him, desperate and panicked as the he watched the Were tear into his arm. The moment seemed to last an eternity as the jaws clame closer, closer, and then began to close on a point mid-way between Albrim's elbow and his shoulder; well above the point his other arm was missing. Frantically he pushed against the beast with his metallic arm but he knew it was too late; he was going to die or worse; survive to live without hands; unable to do even the simplest of tasks for himself. Until he was caught and hung as a Were, of course.

Screaming and wailing as if on fire the Were leaped back from Albrim as two of its teeth fell to the road. The Were had found the silver circlet on Albrim's arm to be less than appetizing. Seeing the fencing foil and hoping that he understood the significance of its lying where it did, Albrim snatched the weapon up and drove it into the Were's flank in an unguarded moment as the creature began changing from his humanoid form to that of a full wolf. Though the weapon was tiny and had little chance of penetrating anything vital at that angle, it did penetrate the Cursed hide and did more than cause a momentary flash of pain. Moaning in fear and agony the beast leapt away, turning away from its former prey and fleeing down the road towards the north; pausing only briefly to rip the throat from a hapless, smaller wolf that had chanced to emerge from the brush and into its path.

Arrows began striking the carriage as wolves appeared in ones and twos along the highway in both directions. The carriage started to move as the draft horses smelled the blood of their former driver and began stomping nervously. With no where else to go, Mute launched another arrow at the nearest wolf before grabbing Albrim by his upper arm and dragging him to his feet. Stooping he next picked up the figure in gray and bodily hurled the light form through a window of the carriage, then forced a staggering Albrim that way with a shove. Clambering up to the driver's seat amidst the rising rain of missiles, Mute kept as low as he could as he snatched up the waiting whip and used it to great effect on the already nervous draft horses. With little provocation they leapt into immediate flight.

Within the carriage Albrim closed the door on the already moving vehicle ahead of several pursuing missiles and crawled to the unmoving Gran. She seemed to be barely breathing and was surely dying from the weight of the Were dropping on her. Frail bones such as hers could never take such pounding and it was nothing short of a miracle that she still lived. In the carriage with him was a human male, small and soft by Albrim's standards, who had managed to pull the body of his dead or dying elven companion into the dubious safety of the vehicle. Albrim could see that the elf was unlikely to survive even if she by chance still lived. A sizeable portion of her skull was missing and the man was covered in her blood.

Albrim looked down at the little woman in his arms. Gran, his only family, the woman that had raised him, rocked him in her arms as an infant and cared for him when he was ill. A woman who had risked everything to give her Cursed grandson a chance at life and now she was dying in his arms. Wanting to look upon her face once more while she still drew breath, Albrim adjusted her weight slightly so that the hood she wore fell back. He was startled to see that her eyes were open.

"Gran?" he said, bewildered that the frail old woman was not only still living, but even conscious.

"Hush, boy," she said, her voice weak as she reached up a shaking hand to pat his face. That task complete she dropped her hand to his good arm and slid it up to his sleeve to feel the bent silver band there before gripping him just below it and giving it a squeeze. Despite her obvious pain and imminent death, she smiled up at her grandson.

"I knew he could help you. Forgive me for sending you away, Albrim. I had to give you a chance for some kind of life."

"You did all that you could for me Gran, all that anyone could have. You've given me life; more than once." Albrim choked, his tears flowing freely. "I love you Gran."

"Hush now, boy. I love you too but you have to listen now. You have to get away, Albrim. You are all that I have. I need you to survive. Everything will have been for nothing if you don't," she whispered, eyes drooping. "It is imperative that you live, promise me..." she demanded, for a moment the old Gran resurfaced but then her voice trailed away, her eyes closed, and she fell back against his support.

"Gran?" demanded Albrim, afraid that she had just died in his arms. Gratefully he saw her thin chest still rose with another breath, but surely she wouldn't last long.

Arrows thumped into the carriage in a continuous tattoo as Albrim glanced from the nearest window. Dozens, perhaps hundreds of Quargs were swarming from the forest amidst a like number of wolves all intent on overtaking the carriage. Just ahead of the carriage came the scream of a horse and the speed of the conveyance slowed. Peering through a small window situated just behind the driver Albrim could see Mute collapsed across the driver's seat, an arrow standing from his ribs. Beyond Mute the draft horses were slowing, neighing in pain and terror from the arrows that protruded from some of their sides. As the horses on the left tried to flee the smell of fresh blood, those on the right were losing strength and beginning to falter. They wouldn't last long. In the air, even through the tiny window, Albrim could see dozens of arrows in flight; most were launched wildly into the trees and even the roadbed; typical Quarg aim when among a group. Enough would be on target to ensure that the horses were doomed, and after them, the occupants of the carriage. Mute could already be dead.

Albrim searched for an escape, any avenue to get himself and his loved ones away. Could they leap from the carriage before it stopped completely? Not likely; Mute was too large for him to move and Gran would never survive the impact of the fall. Only he was healthy enough to make the attempt but he couldn't find the strength to go and leave Gran behind. Even if they did jump, he certainly couldn't outrun the Quargs and even if he tried to hide from them the wolves would track him down in short order. They were all doomed.

"There has to be something," Albrim snarled, slamming his fist into the thick carpet of the floor. He tried to think but all he could bring to mind was Gran's words; perhaps her last words, begging him to escape.

"I've got to do something," he raged, looking back at Gran's face; she was so still, so quiet. "Flee boy," she seemed to beg. "Save yourself, don't be a hero."

As he watched her face Albrim was surprised to see his tears dripping on Gran's face. Were she awake he knew she'd be scolding him; ordering him to jump from the carriage and escape. "You have to get away," she had said.

Should he go? Should he flee? Gran wanted him to go; to live, to survive. Mute would have simply picked him up and thrown him out. Both of the people he cared about wanted him to live, to run away like a coward. Is that what he was? Albrim knew that he was no hero; he'd accepted that someone with the Curse could never be a hero; never be someone others looked up to but could he live with himself if he abandoned Gran and Mute now?

Gasping in sudden pain Albrim looked to see an arrow had passed through a window and struck him in the thigh. Blood quickly stained his clothing and began to soak into the carpet; the pain fueling the rage he already felt. Albrim screamed then; a deep, primal roar of pain, fear, and hatred at those who would kill him. Though he didn't see it one of the draft horses collapsed at the moment his scream began, causing the poor beasts behind it to trip. It was almost as if time had stopped or at least slowed down as the carriage tipped up on one set of wheels, one of which snapped from the weight, and then rolled over.

The world turned upside down then as new flashes of pain blasted through both Albrim's head and his good arm as he found himself somehow thrown from the wreckage. He skidded across the edge of the road and into the ditch on that side; the brambles and thorns of the brush ripping at him, tearing long strips of skin from his face and arms even as his leg wound sprayed blood in an arc around him. More pain ripped through his guts, hinting at injuries he could not imagine the extent of as he clawed and bit at the grass in his agony.

"Run away, boy," Gran screamed at him. The words existed only in his agonized mind but years of obedience forced him into motion. Grabbing at the bole of a sapling, Albrim somehow staggered to his feet and began to run from the war horns of the Quargs and the howls of the wolves, leaving behind Gran, Mute and the Viscount to the mercy of the evil humanoids. Uppermost on his mind was escaping the horrible pain, the agony that pummeled him and threatened to tear his mind from his head and to obey the memory of Gran's last command. Albrim didn't know that he was screaming from the pain.

Albrim didn't make it far; the arrow through his thigh caused his weakened leg to collapse under the strain. More waves of agony passed through, beginning somewhere near his toes and rippling through his body, wracking him with spasms to leave him convulsing about on the ground as white foam began to form at the corners of his mouth. His screams drew the attention of wolves and Quargs alike, who began to gather about him in awe as he thrashed about in the underbrush, every muscle in his body on fire.

Albrim's last sight as consciousness faded was of a gigantic, growling wolf leaning over him, the spittle from its muzzle dripping on his upturned face.

Epilogue

Captain Ilrod of the Fifth Royal Horse led his troops along the highway that dawn, aghast at the carnage they had discovered. Even the most veteran of his warriors were sickened by the blood and body parts scattered about the highway. A score or more Quargs lay where they had fallen and at least that many wolves lay in pieces as well. Whatever had killed them had not been thorough; ripping off limbs or biting large chunks of flesh from its prey and leaving them to bleed slowly to death on the road. Later it had returned to feed, choosing its meals from among those who still lived.

As they neared the wreckage of an overturned carriage the Captain help up a hand and called a halt, then ordered four men to dismount to search for survivors in the conveyance and detailed the others to search the Quargs as his best trackers tried to make sense of the jumble of footprints along the edges of the road. It didn't take the men long to report the lack of survivors.

"The carriage is empty, Captain, but blood is splattered everywhere. All the mounts are dead as well; some by Quarg arrows and two were mauled. I'd say it was the wolves, sir," Lead Scout Orzik reported, kicking the severed head of a wolf that in life would have been easily the size of a pony. "Whoever was in the carriage was either carried off by the Quargs or eaten."

The Captain looked at the corpses; some were so mauled as to be indistinguishable as Quarg, human, or any other race for that matter.

"Join the others, Orzik, see if you can find someone alive to tell us what happened," the Captain ordered.

"Sir!" shouted a man searching the flattened brush along the eastern side of the road. The warrior was holding up something shiny for his Captain to see.

"Bring it here, warrior," ordered the Captain, urging his horse a little closer but trying to keep it from stepping in the spread pools of dried blood. They were trained war horses but you never knew when one might spook. Having advanced as far as he intended to, the Captain watched as the youthful warrior carefully stepped over the corpses of the big dray horses to reach his commander's side.

"I found this, Captain, crushed down in the underbrush. It must have fallen out of the wagon, or was thrown out. I only saw it because the sun glinted off of it."

The Captain accepted the blood-covered object uneasily, recognizing it as silver despite the deep brown color it currently bore. It was circular in shape with a series of glyphs on the inside and nothing but a small ax head engraved on the outside.

"Odd, I've never seen anything like this before," the Captain mused as he stowed the object into his saddle bag. If no one claimed it the silver would fetch a nice price in Aldragal. "Anything else?"

"Some papers, Captain," offered a second warrior, holding up a leather satchel. "This one here looks like a patent of nobility," he finished, pulling a single sheet of vellum from the bag. Ilrod knew the man couldn't read, but once he perused the papers himself he knew the man had made a good guess.

"The Viscount of Gelbow," he read, the name partially obscured by blood. "All right men, lets see what else we can find," he added, looking greedily towards the gemstones visible on the carriage.

From the forest an animal watched the patrol searching the wreckage with minimal interest. Sated from a night of feeding on the fresh blood and flesh of so many enemies, the Were thought of little now except sleeping off its engorged belly. It felt safe enough from the humans and there was a lot more of the slow-moving and weak prey hiding in the woods around. Tonight the Were would feed again. There was no hurry.

About the Author

Trevis Powell was born in rural Howevalley Kentucky and resides there with his wife and four children. After spending his school-age years more interested in sports than grades, he followed a six-year stint in the U.S. Army Reserves with various manual-labor intensive jobs. Eventually he went back to college, earning a degree in electronics.

After his marriage he settled down in his hometown and his creative desire, something he had dealt with since he was a teenager, finally became too strong to ignore and he began to write. Reading, and later gaming, had become outlets for his creative side and he noticed that his adventure designs and gaming worlds were always far more detailed than necessary to play a simple game. Over time these became even more elaborate, and he finally had to admit that he needed more. Falling back on his natural story-telling ability he began to experiment with writing.

Two years later Trevis found his first publisher in Elmore Productions. Over the next five years he saw his name in print in a variety of outlets, including short stories, magazines, and gaming material. Again he found that he wanted more; feeling the need to develop the stories and characters he invented in greater detail. Now focusing on novels, Trevis is proud to be among the first authors in the new Blackwyrm Fiction line.

Also from BlackWyrm...

by Ian Harac

One FBI agent
One geekette
One dead munchkin
Parallel worlds galore
An interdimensional conspiracy.
When Matt Anders stumbles
across the body of a dead
munchkin in a suspect's
apartment, a conspiracy begins to
unravel that leads him on a
reality-jumping adventure to the
magical Land of Oz... and beyond!
[Snarky SciFi Thriller, ages 14+]

by Brad Parnell

Young Robert journeys to another
world. There he comes of age amid
a feuding government, grotesque
monsters, an ancient ancestor
...and a couple of teenaged girls.
With the help of a young wolf
named Louie, Robert is introduced
to the wonders and perils of a
strange land called Gwerinatha.
[Allegoric Celtic Fantasy, ages 12+]

by Jason Walters

At the edge of the known world, two desperate armies struggle for the right to siege a city that has never been taken. Terrible magics are unleashed and the fate of empires hangs in the balance. Highdome and his crew of cutthroats, monsters, and mutants don't care. They just want to stay alive. But when sorcery backfires and the fury of the Vast White desert is unleashed, the men and women of the Red Regiment must look inside of themselves to find the strength to survive.
[Dark Military Fantasy, ages 14+]

by Dirk Vandereyken

In a small village, a necromancer stands trial. At the center of the universe, the Spider that wove All watches intently. Webs are spun in the courtroom, of magic, of lies, and of scandal. The mage Baour argues that he supercedes not only man's laws, but god's! What he truly wants may only be uncovered through testimony. As strange magics meet strange deaths, can the reality behind it be unmasked? And should it?
[Fantasy Legal Thriller, ages 18+]

AFTERTHOUGHTS
by Lynn Tincher

Detective Paige Aldridge was found beaten and without any memories of the previous few months. When her nephew is found dead a year later, she begins to have terrifying flashbacks, plus visions of the murders of her own family! As her loved ones begin falling prey to a serial killer, Paige believes that she must be going mad. With her family dying around her and dark suspicions forming in her mind, Paige has to pull the pieces together before it's too late. [Psychic Crime Thriller, ages 14+]

LEFT IN THE DARK
by Lynn Tincher

Paige's adventures continue as she learns more of her developing powers, while she deepens her relationships with her partner and her sister. Can she regain control of her own mind before the powers that threaten to tear her apart claim her sanity and the life of a ten year old girl? Past, present, and future all collide with fear in this chilling sequel. [Psychic Crime Thriller, ages 14+]